You Also May Enjoy These Other Books
by
Theodore Jerome Cohen

*Death by Wall Street**
*House of Cards**
*Lilith**
*Night Shadows**
*Eighth Circle**
*Wheel of Fortune**
Frozen in Time†
Unfinished Business†
End Game†
Cold Blood††
Full Circle
The Hypnotist‡ ‡‡
The Road Less Taken – Books 1 & 2
Creative Ink, Flashy Fiction – Books 1, 2, 3, 4, 5 & 6
Flash Fiction for Animal Lovers (Anthology Book 7)
Flash Fiction Stories of the Young (Anthology Book 8)
*Flash Fiction Stories for the Warrior (Anthology Book 9)***
*Flash Fiction Stories with a Feminine Twist (Anthology Book 10)***
*Flash Fiction Stories with a Masculine Twist (Anthology Book 11)***
*Flash Fiction Stories for the Religiously Inclined (Anthology Book 12)***
*Flash Fiction Stories Musically Inclined (Anthology Book 13)***
*Flash Fiction Stories of the Sea (Anthology Book 14)***
Mementos (Anthology Books 1, 2, & 3)

* A Detective Louis Martelli, NYPD, Mystery/Thriller
† The Antarctic Murders Trilogy
†† The Antarctic Murders Trilogy (all three books in one volume)
‡ Young Adult (YA) novel written under the pen name "Alyssa Devine"
‡‡ Also available in a special paperback edition for readers with dyslexia
** Contains some short stories

Visit us on the World Wide Web
http://www.theodore-cohen-novels.com
http://www.alyssadevinenovels.com

Flash Fiction Stories
for Students and Teachers

Book 15 in the <u>Flash Fiction Anthologies</u> Series

Theodore Jerome Cohen
Alyssa Devine

TJC Press

TJC Press
122 Shady Brook Drive
Langhorne, PA 19047-8027 USA
www.theodore-cohen-novels.com
© Theodore Jerome Cohen, 2021 • All rights reserved

*The stories in this book are works of fiction, though some were inspired by real events. Except as noted in the **Endnotes**, which are made a part of this declaration, any resemblance to actual persons (living or dead), events, or locales in the context of the stories presented here, is coincidental. All brand names and product names used in this book are trademarks, registered trademarks, or trade names of their respective holders.*

Some stories first appeared as submissions to Flash Fiction Challenges sponsored by Indies Unlimited (www.IndiesUnlimited.com); these were inspired by copyrighted photographic prompts provided by K. S. Brooks that were originally posted at Indies Unlimited.

Book 15 in the series, <u>Flash Fiction Anthologies</u>
First Edition; First Printing, 2021
ISBN-13: 9798521880423 (sc)

Published in the United States of America
Front cover design by Theodore Jerome Cohen
*The paperback edition is printed using THE DOVES TYPE® typeface, Robert Green's digital recreation of the Doves Press Fount of Type. See **Endnote 1** for more information.*
https://typespec.co.uk/doves-type/

Photo Credits
Front cover art: RTimages, Big Stock Photo
Frontispiece: Big Stock Photo
Photograph of Theodore Jerome Cohen: Susan Cohen, 2006
Photograph of Alyssa Devine: Big Stock Photo
Photographic prompts copyrighted by K. S. Brooks are used with permission. The copyright or other attribution associated with any given photographic prompt (e.g., royalty-free acquisitions from Big Stock Photo; public domain; etc.) is provided with that prompt. Please provide documented proof of any errors or omissions in, or any changes requested to, these prompts (e.g., changes resulting from inadvertent copyright violations), by letter, to TJC Press.

eBook created by Kindle Direct Publishing (KDP)
Printed by KDP, An Amazon.com Company
Available from Amazon.com and other retail outlets

Because of the dynamic nature of the Internet, any Web addresses or links contained in this book may have changed since publication and may no longer be valid. The views expressed in this work are solely those of the authors.

To Robert "Bob" Suchy, my Riverside High School,
Milwaukee, Wisconsin, homeroom teacher (1953 – 1956),
who put me on my life's path
in science and engineering

"Whatever the cost of our libraries, the price is cheap
compared to that of an ignorant nation."

Walter Cronkite

Table of Contents

A Note from Theodore Jerome Cohen

Marian Wright Edelman said: "Education is for improving the lives of others and for leaving your community and world better than you found it." Lending credence to these words are many of the 38 stories here about students and teachers. The tales, both serious and humorous, were selected from among the 438 stories found in Books 1 through 6, incl., of the authors' *Creative Ink, Flashy Fiction* anthologies. Included as well are selected offerings from Cohen's two short-story anthologies, *The Road Less Taken*, from his *Mementos* series of anthologies, and, in one case, an excerpt from a chapter of one of Cohen's mystery/thrillers. This anthology is unique because the stories were inspired by photographic prompts that were related by Cohen to students and teachers. whether they be in high school or college settings, in classroom or campus situations, or even absent from the scene altogether, here, for example, the subject of a murder investigation.

Some of the stories found here were entered into Flash Fiction Challenges managed by the Website *Indies Unlimited.* In a nutshell, the Challenges (which begin every Saturday morning at 9 a.m., Pacific time) require participants to write a complete story (plot, characters, hook, and slam-bang finish) in 250 words or fewer. Each must incorporate the elements of a photographic and written prompt. Language and subject matter must be kept at the PG-13 level.[1] Entries are accepted until Tuesday at 5:00 p.m., with the winner announced on the following Saturday.

Weekly winners, selected by popular vote, receive the "Flash Fiction Star." Another weekly winner, "Editors' Choice," is selected by the administrators/editors for inclusion in an annual anthology. Announcements of the latter can lag submission by several months.

---

1 You can learn more at <u>www.indiesunlimited.com/flash-fiction/</u>

"Alyssa Devine" is a pen name I use when writing Young Adult (YA) novels and some other literature. Know, then, that I sometimes submitted stories for consideration in the *Indies Unlimited* competitions in her name, just for the fun of it. You'll also find original stories by "Alyssa" in this anthology.

The majority of the stories here were inspired by interesting or unusual photographs found on the Internet. And if some of the stories appear somewhat obtuse, read their associated endnotes. You may be surprised at what inspired a given tale.

So, without further ado, I give you this, "our" 14th collection of flash fiction. Just don't ingest the stories too quickly. They're best savored in small helpings.

Theodore Jerome Cohen
aka Alyssa Devine
Langhorne, Pennsylvania
June 16, 2021

NB: The paperback edition of this book is printed using THE DOVES TYPE® typeface, Robert Green's digital recreation of the Doves Press Fount of Type. See **Endnote** 1 for more information on this typeface and its tortured history.

Acknowledgements

I will forever be grateful to my wife, Susan (1943 – 2021)—the love of my life—who provided vital suggestions and, equally important, unswerving support, during the development of my writings.

Those we love don't go away,
they walk beside us every day.
Unheard but always near,
still loved, still missed, and very dear.

I don't know what I am going to do without you.

Flash Fiction Stories
for Students and Teachers

Flash Fiction Anthology – Book 15

"On Making Coffee and Other Endeavors"
(Photo: By permission of the Department of Geoscience, University of
Wisconsin-Madison. Appreciation is expressed to Emeritus Professor Robert
H. Dott, Jr., PhD, Department of Geoscience, University of Wisconsin-
Madison, for his assistance in obtaining this photo
and for permission to use it here.)

Professor Richard Conrad Emmons (1898-1993), a member of the
University of Wisconsin-Madison Department of Geology faculty for 45
years. The only thing "Con" valued more than a good cup of coffee was
a student's curiosity.

1. On Making Coffee and Other Endeavors

Theodore Jerome Cohen

As usual, University of Wisconsin-Madison Professor Jonathan Conrad Fairclouth III was late for his 8 a.m. Monday morning class on Advanced Paleontology. In fact, his students, current and otherwise, could not remember his *ever* having arrived on time for *any* class, often stretching the obligatory 20-minute waiting period for a tenured professor to the very last second. Now, with a minute to go and the students in his Geology 205a lecture section beginning to pack their books and laptop computers, Fairclouth appeared, lecture notes grasped firmly in his left hand, a porcelain coffee mug emblazoned with Bucky Badger held tightly in his right.

To the professor, coffee was more than a morning staple. Brewing it was a ritual and the liquid itself—the "nectar of the gods," as Fairclouth called it— was something to be savored. So, as was his practice, the first order of business, the *very* first thing discussed at the beginning of every lecture, was that morning's brew and the precise process by which it had been prepared.

"I tried a new blend this morning," he intoned with a twinkle in his eyes. The students perked up. Some knew that look. They had seen it last semester when Fairclouth substituted crystals he had made using maple candy for one specimen on a mineral identification quiz.

"Kopi luwak coffee!" he blurted out. "That's the key!"

"Oh boy," Mary Wilson muttered under her breath, raising her eyebrows. A senior intent on pursuing a career in petroleum engineering, she gave everyone in the class a run for their money, both academically and physically. Smart, attractive, and a former star of Washington High School's track team in Milwaukee, she'd already been accepted for postgraduate work by the Colorado School of Mines, where she intended to pursue a doctorate.

"What?" asked Jarod Sanger, who was sitting to her right and still half-asleep after a weekend of barhopping on State Street.

Wilson leaned toward him, and covering her mouth with her right hand, whispered, "The coffee he's drinking . . . it's made from beans that have passed through the digestive systems of Asian palm civets. The stuff is unbelievably expensive."

Sanger made a face of a youngster who had just been given castor oil. "Are you f—?"

Wilson put her right forefinger on her classmate's lips, stopping not only his outburst but more importantly, the possibility Fairclouth might single them both out for special attention. Fortunately, the professor had moved on, and by the time the two turned their attention back to the podium, Fairclouth already was discussing the brewing process he had used that morning, including a review of his lab-quality borosilicate glass percolator, the water's characteristics—filtered, neither distilled nor softened—and the precise percolation time needed for the finely ground kopi luwak coffee. In addition, he reviewed how, precisely, he had ground the beans to the point where the coffee would pass through a #40 sieve. He left nothing out. Not one detail.

The students had heard much the same before. As a captive audience, however, they could do nothing but sit in silence while the "master" waxed poetic on the joys of brewing this morning's cup o' joe.

It drove them crazy! It also chewed up the first 10 minutes of the class. And given the professor had arrived 20 minutes late, whatever he had to say now on the topic of advanced paleontology would have to be squeezed into the remaining 20 minutes of the 50-minute period.

Not that the professor cared. Learning the material wasn't *his* problem. He knew it. And the textbook he had selected, together with the supplemental notes he had distributed on the first day of class, were more than sufficient to give students the knowledge they needed to pass the quizzes and final exam from which their grades would be determined.

But this was only part of the story, only part of what made Professor Jonathan Conrad Fairclouth III "tick." What he valued most was a student's *curiosity*. Whom he sought out were those who thrived on acquiring knowledge—not because they were under some compulsion to learn but because they truly were inspired by something they had read, heard him say, or observed in class.

"Give me a curious student," he would say, "and I will give you a valued member of society." True to his word, some of today's leaders in academia—specifically in the fields of sedimentology, stratigraphy, stratigraphic paleontology, and X-ray crystallography, among other disciplines—and in industry—specifically in such commercial enterprises as geophysical exploration, mining, and oil and gas extraction—earned their master's and doctoral degrees under his direction.

This is not to say the concept of time, in and of itself, was not important to Professor Fairclouth. The subjects of his innumerable studies, experiments, scientific papers, and lectures spanned hundreds of millions of years of geologic time. In particular, he devoted a good portion of his life to the study of curled-shelled creatures known as ammonites, which lived from the Devonian Period to the Cretaceous Period (roughly from between 420 million and 65 million years ago). Perhaps because of this enormous expanse of time, something few can even wrap their heads around, you got the feeling a few minutes here or there were of no importance whatsoever to the professor. And you'd be correct. If he didn't finish a lecture today, there'd always be another in two or three days. "What's the rush?" he'd ask if someone attempted to move things along. "Everything in due time."

According to some of his colleagues, Fairclouth would have been just as happy if time stood still. It was true. In many ways the man was an anachronism, from the way he dressed—he delivered his lectures at this time of year in a tweed suit, starched white shirt, and bow tie—to what he drove: a white, 1983, meticulously maintained Chrysler New Yorker with 14,000 miles on the odometer. The actual mileage was 114,000, but the mechanism on the console displayed only the last five digits.

This penchant for taking a *laissez-faire* attitude towards time was such that he maintained what many considered the old-fashioned concept of an "open door" policy toward visitors, one in which a student—any student, whether his or not—was welcome to drop in at any time and discuss anything with the professor, no matter the subject, no matter the time required. Unlike many of his colleagues, Fairclouth wasn't one to hide in the field or lab or to shirk his classroom responsibilities by declining to teach certain courses because, selfishly, he wanted to pursue his research. To him, teaching was, first and foremost, a responsibility to be taken seriously. More to the point, to him it was a sacred responsibility.

So, having missed a few classes in which the professor discussed the ammonites of the Devonian Period—those that lived more than 400 million years ago—I trundled off one early October afternoon to the Lewis Weeks Hall for Geological Sciences, intending to engage the good professor in a discussion about the creatures.

I found him hunched behind his massive weather-beaten walnut desk in a corner office not more than 12 feet square, an office covered from floor to ceiling with bookshelves that overflowed with, and sagged under the weight of, a ton of scientific and scholarly journals, periodicals, and publications from all over the world. An old pendulum schoolhouse clock kept time on the wall next to the office's only window, which, though somewhat grimy, framed a courtyard looking splendid in its full fall regalia.

The room's atmosphere was quite agreeable. A large glass ashtray on the left side of the desk held two pipes. In it, ashes still smoldered with the faint scent of the aromatic blend of tobaccos the professor smoked. Below the ashtray was a stack of scientific reprints, each endorsed, I'm sure, with the obligatory "With the compliments of the author" scribbled in the upper-right-hand corner. A rolled-up copy of Madison's *The Capital Times* had been unceremoniously dumped into the wastepaper basket. God forbid he used the same container for the contents of his ashtray, something I'm sure must have concerned both the department staff and the building custodians.

Behind him, on the credenza, were various scientific awards and research instruments. "Never buy what you can make," he would tell his lab students, pointing with pride at the various devices he had designed and fabricated, some with the help of master machinists in the university's machine shop. A prolific author, he was always in the process of penning—and I do mean *penning*, with ink pen and paper—one scientific paper or another if not acting as a reviewer for major geological journals in the United States, Canada, and Europe.

And still, though you might think the pressures from his teaching and other obligations would have driven him into a frenzy, I found him to be the very picture of serenity. Perhaps it was the absence of a computer in his office, though there certainly was one on virtually everyone else's desk in the department. His desk phone—there was no cell phone in sight, nor had I ever seen him use one—was of simple construction, with three push-buttons on the console below the touch-tone keypad: two for incoming lines and one for call holding. For all intents and purposes, the office really had not changed—*had not evolved*—in form or function for decades. In it, time had stood still. To my eyes, it could just as easily have been a day in 1975 as it was now, in 1995.

He was oblivious to my presence, so I knocked softly on the door jamb.

Fairclouth's head jerked at the sound. Looking up, he recognized me instantly. "Come in, come in," he beckoned, setting down a paper he had been reviewing and putting his red pen aside. "How can I help you?"

I explained the purpose of my visit. He was delighted, ammonites being among his favorite topics.

"Of course. Let's chat." The professor opened the lower right-hand drawer of his desk and extracted a folder from which he withdrew a photograph of an ammonite from the Devonian Period. The coiled shell in the photograph—it looked a lot like the modern nautilus—had been carefully sliced open, revealing in plan view the creature's internal structure. It was partitioned into a collection of adjoining chambers, each separated by a wall which, in this case, was slightly curved.

"Isn't she a beauty? Lived in shallow marine waters, she did. See the simple suture pattern?" He pointed to the pattern that marked where the internal partitioning walls intersected the outer shell.

"You can't miss these suture marks, they're easily recognizable. In this case, of course, they're very simple . . . we're in the Devonian."

These creatures were a thing of beauty, all right. It was easy for me to understand why the professor was so taken with them.

"They make great index fossils, you know," he continued as he pulled another photograph from the folder. "They're found everywhere, you know, so they can be used for dating the rocks in which they're found."

He handed me the second photograph. *This is interesting,* I thought as I studied it. The crenulated and complex sutures I observed in the shell of the second ammonite stood in sharp contrast to the simple sutures of the first specimen. I almost did a double-take.

Fairclouth laughed. "Caught you by surprise, didn't it?"

"Well, I certainly wasn't expecting such a remarkable change."

"They did evolve rapidly, that's for sure," he said. "Makes them a great help in dating marine rocks. This one is from the Triassic Period—about 250 million years ago."

It was easy to understand the love he had for the field from the way he looked lovingly at the photographs and spoke of the creatures.

The old clock chimed once, but Professor Fairclouth evidenced no sign of having heard it. I knew we both had obligations: I, a 1 p.m. lecture in a course on Sedimentology and Stratigraphy on the building's 2nd floor; he, a two-hour lab on Tidal Sedimentation to be conducted in the building's basement. Neither of us rose.

"Now," he said, almost proudly, "look at this one."

The photograph he thrust into my hand was that of an ammonite from the Cretaceous Period. The label at the bottom clearly showed the creature was dated to 70 million years ago. The suture marks—that is, the marks where the internal partitioning walls intersected the outer shell—were highly crenulated and complex, full of all manner of twists and swirls.

Neither of us said anything for a minute. Finally, smiling wryly, he asked, "Do you think there might be more here than meets the eye?"

I hesitated. The professor was known to have a good heart. It wasn't his nature to draw a student into a trap, only to use a question such as this as a pretense to demonstrate his superior knowledge or embarrass the novice. "Well," I ventured timidly, "it took 330 million years, give or take, but it would appear that, as time progressed, things got more and more complex until, in the end, the organism became extinct."

"Bingo!" cried the professor. "So, why is everyone in such a hurry these days to speed things up, to add complexity to their lives when it all can come to no good end? Relax. Life is short. Enjoy what you have. Take time to 'be in the moment.'"

He looked at the clock on the wall. "I know, I know . . . you thought I'd forgotten about my next class, didn't you?" He chuckled. "Well, I still have a good 10 minutes before they pack up and leave." With that, he rose, grabbed some notes from his desk, and pushed his chair back.

"Don't you have somewhere to be?" he asked as he turned toward the door.

"Oh, I guess. But you know, I never was able to take your course in Tidal Sedimentation—I simply couldn't work it into my schedule. Do you mind if I sit in on today's lab session? Just out of curiosity, of course?"

"Set a Place for Sister Margaret" (Photo: Sophie Madson, Pinterest)

"Have Sister Mary set a place for Sister Margaret at dinner. She will arrive Milwaukee, 6 p.m., tonight, via Badger Bus."

2. Set a Place for Sister Margaret

Theodore Jerome Cohen

(non-fiction)

According to Ken Eggert, W9MOT, then-president of the Milwaukee Radio Amateur Club, the call came from the Roman Catholic Archdiocese of Milwaukee, Wisconsin. "They need someone to act as a go-between for Queen of Apostles Seminary in Madison and St. Anthony's in Milwaukee. Your contact in Madison, Ted, would be a priest . . . Father John Haas. His call sign is W9UJF."

It was easy to understand why the Church might want such an arrangement. After all, the year was 1953. Those were the days when AT&T was the only long-distance telephone company in the US. Calls to distant places were extremely expensive. Even calls between Milwaukee and Madison, if placed on a frequent basis, produced high monthly bills. A free communication link to pass messages between parties in distant cities was something out of a dream!

I had received my Novice Amateur Radio license with the callsign WN9VZL just four months earlier, in November, 1952. So it came as a surprise the club's president thought of me as the person to help.

"This requires someone who is available every weekday. All you have to do is get on the air after school for about 10 minutes," he continued, "copy any messages Father Haas has for St. Anthony's, send him whatever 'traffic' St. Anthony's has for the seminary, and that's it. I know you can do it. Waddaya think?"

"But I only can use code," I protested. At that time, Novices on the shortwave bands were limited to using Morse code (strictly speaking, the International Morse code).

Unfortunately, my receiving speed was 5 words per minute, just enough to pass the code test required by the FCC. "If I'm going to do this, Father Hass will have to use code as well. I hope he's a patient man."

Ken laughed. "I've already spoken to Father John. He's looking forward to working with you."

Thus began a friendship that extended throughout my high school years and beyond. Our on-air schedules, at 4:30 p.m. sharp, were conducted with military precision:

> "WN9VZL de W9UJF Hi, Ted. Pls cl St
> A. Hv Sister Mary set place 4 Sister
> Margaret at dinner. She wl arrve
> Milw 6 pm 2nite via Badger Bus. AR
> K"
> "W9UJF de WN9VZL RR Nil frm St A.
> AR K"
> "WN9VZL de W9UJF Tnx es 73 AR SK"
> "73 CL"

And with that farewell, we both closed our stations.

When school was not in session, we met Mondays, Wednesdays, and Fridays.

On it went for more than three years, two hams, communicating, day in and day out, *without ever having met*. This was and still is the magic of ham radio. It mattered not that one was a Palatine priest and the other a Jewish high school student. We were, simply, John and Ted. Our common bond was ham radio. Our 'language' was the Morse code.

Then, one Saturday afternoon in late winter, 1956, the doorbell rang. Peering out, and to my great surprise, I saw a priest. He smiled and waved. Instantly I knew it must be John. Once inside, we sat in the living room eating cookies while hurrying to catch up on the previous three years of our lives.

Talk ranged from our daily contacts, to our equipment and antennas, to the sunspot numbers and the improving radio conditions . . . and to the matzoh ball soup my mother was cooking for Passover.

"I *love* matzoh ball soup!" John proclaimed. "I can't get food like that in the seminary." Hearing that, my mother presented him with a bowl of hot soup and matzoh balls, forever cementing the relationship between the House of Cohen, Milwaukee, and Queen of Apostles Seminary, Madison. The look on Father John's face said it all.

Only after he had a second helping did talk again turn to our first love: radio.

See Endnote 2.

"Falls" (Photo: K. S. Brooks)
Yaak River, Idaho
Indies Unlimited, June 3, 2017

"Best I can tell she must have conjured up memories of the floating valley with the river running through it—you know, the river that formed into various waterfalls."

3. Falls

Theodore Jerome Cohen

"You seem 'down' these days, Charles. Is something wrong?"
There was no response.
"Charles! Did you hear me?"

"I'm sorry, Reverend. It's been a very difficult few days. Ever since we returned from our last outing, the dean pretty well has let it be known he doesn't want me anywhere near his children."

"Are you sure about that?"

"Oh, yes. I think it's because I upset Alice. I know our last picnic in the forest was a bit difficult for her. Best I can tell she must have conjured up memories of the floating valley with the river running through it—you know, the river that formed into various waterfalls."

"But children do that. They magnify things, sometimes 'way out of proportion."

"I know, my friend, I know—but I've never seen her so upset. And all her tears did was get Edith upset, too. God only knows what they told their parents after we dropped them off. Perhaps the stories we've been making up are too scary, though Lorina should be old enough to understand them."

"I don't think the stories are the problem, Charles, at least as far as the dean is concerned."

"What are you talking about?"

The reverend hesitated, but then, in a soft voice, said what he and Charles both knew was the nub of the matter. "I think the dean and his wife are concerned that Lorina has a crush on you."

See Endnote 3.

"Einstein" (Photo: Pinterest)

"So, today's your birthday."

4. Einstein

Theodore Jerome Cohen

"**So,** today's your birthday?"

"Yes. March 14th, a day that will live 'in family'." [He laughs.]

"That's cute. Did you make that up?"

"Heavens, no! My grandfather kicked the slats out of his cradle the first time he heard it."

"But you did say that the definition of insanity is doing the same thing over and over and expecting different results, right?"

"Oh my . . . never said that either. I think Rita Mae Brown might claim credit for that, but in any event, that's not the definition of insanity. What you're dealing with there is a psychosis so debilitating that a person can't distinguish fantasy from reality."

"Well, what about this quote: 'Everyone is a genius. But if you judge a fish by its ability to climb a tree, it will live its whole life believing it is stupid.'? That sounds like something you might have said."

"Nope, wasn't me," he said, picking up his violin and tuning the instrument.

"Well then, are you familiar with this one: 'I refuse to believe that God plays dice with the universe.'?"

"Close, but no cigar. What I actually wrote my friend Cornelius Lanczos at Princeton in 1942 was: 'It seems hard to sneak a look at God's cards. But that He plays dice . . . is something I cannot believe for a single moment.'"

"So, what can we believe you said?"

"Just this: 'Don't believe every quote you read on the Internet, because I totally didn't say that.'"

"Youth" (Photo: Pinterest)

"Do you remember this picture, Bill?"

5. Youth

Theodore Jerome Cohen

"**Do** you remember this picture, Bill?"

"Let me think. That's you holding the ball, of course, and me to your right. I'm sure that's Marty—Martin Graves—on your left. Correct?"

"You got a good memory. D'you recall when it was taken?"

[He laughs.] "Gimme a break, Charlie. At my age, you're lucky I could even name everyone in the picture.

"Well, according to my Mom's writing on the back, it was March, 1931. Coulda guessed it was late winter or early spring by the fact we're playing ball in those clothes. But what the hell was Marty doing, running around like that?"

"Beats me. Jesus, 'e always was the wild one, wasn't 'e? Crazy as they come. I thought 'e was going to drive Sister Theresa up a tree, the way 'e misbehaved in school. I think she spent half 'er time taking a ruler to 'is hand, but it never made one whit of difference. Back 'e came the next day for more."

"I know. It made me cringe when she marched up the aisle, tapping 'er ruler on the palm of 'er left hand before stopping at 'is desk. And then, WHACK! Right on the top of 'is hand. Not once, but two or three times until it turned a bright red. You could see tears welling up in 'is eyes, but 'e never cried. Not once."

"I know. 'E was a good kid. 'E didn't deserve to die on Omaha Beach."

"Dog" (Photo: Pinterest/piccsy)

"Aw, come on, I didn't mean no harm, Joey."

6. Dog

Theodore Jerome Cohen

"Aw, come on, I didn't mean no harm, Joey."

"I'm not done being angry with you yet!"

"Hey, I'm supposed to be your best friend, ya know."

"Who sez? I don't believe it anymore after what you did."

"Well, it's true. We have a long history of great relations with humans. For one thing, we're loyal. And look at the great companionship we provide. Who keeps you warm on those cold winter nights by sleeping on your feet? Now answer me that?! Even Frederick the Great loved us."

"Yeah, well, Frederick the Great didn't have to put up with a mutt like you."

"Hey, that hurt, Joey. We've been a team since the people you call 'Mom' and 'Dad' brought you home from the hospital, right? Remember how I used to grab your diaper to keep you from falling down the stairs? Whew, it sure stank! But did I let that stop me? No, sir. I saved you again and again. 'Mom' and 'Dad' appreciated that. But here you are, making those awful statements about me after all the times I saved your life."

"Yeah, well then, tell me why I get these poor grades."

[Dog looks confused.]

"I'll tell you why. Because every time I leave my homework next to my book bag, I come back to find you've eaten it. That's why!"

"Playboy" (Photo: Pinterest)

"Ethan, where are you?"

7. Playboy
Theodore Jerome Cohen

"Ethan, where are you?"

"On the porch, Ma!"

"Whaddaya doing out there in the hot sun?"

"I'm reading, Ma! Didn't ya always tell me to read during the summer to improve my language skills?"

"Why, yes, I did, Ethan. I'm proud of you, son."

A minute of silence goes by.

"My, you're awful quiet out there. You must be reading something very interesting. What it is?"

"It's a literary magazine, Ma. One of the best available. I got it from Johnnie . . . it's his father's—you know, the lawyer?"

"Oh, well then, it must be an exceptional magazine. Is there anything in particular you find interesting?"

There is an almost imperceptible sound of pages being turned as Ethan thumbs through the publication.

"Ethan? Did you hear me?"

"Yes, Ma, I heard you! I was just engrossed in this short story by Roald Dahl . . . something about a woman who, after being widowed, reconnects with the man she had left for her former husband years before. It's called 'The Last Act.' Very good, I must say."

"Well, thank God you're not reading one of those awful magazines with pictures of naked women in them, that's all I can say."

"Cheating" (Photo: Pinterest)

"Keep looking up at the ceiling so Old Man Bick
doesn't see us talking."

8. Cheating

Theodore Jerome Cohen

"**P**sst! Kit! Can you hear me?"

[Low voice.] "Yeah, whaddaya want, Nick?"

"Keep looking up at the ceiling so Old Man Bick doesn't see us talking."

"Got it."

"I see you're having trouble with the math problem, too."

"Yeah . . . it doesn't make sense to me:

```
If a train at Point A heads north at 60 miles
per hour, and another train on the same track,
90 miles to the north at Point B, heads south
at 30 miles per hour, how long will it take for
them to meet?
```

"Do you understand it, Nick?"

"Naw. Where does he get these problems, anyway?"

"Who cares? You should see *my* train."

"Really? Whaddaya have, Kit?"

"My Dad's old Lionel set, from when he was a kid—it includes the 2023 Union Pacific Alco AA diesels in yellow and gray, together with the Plainfield and Westfield Pullmans and the Livingston observation car."

"Neato-torpedo!"

"What about you?"

"My dad has an American Flyer set we bring out every Christmas—the 4901 'Atlantic'-type freight train, with a boxcar, coal car, and caboose. The use of two tracks makes things look very realistic. And the train even makes a 'choo-choo' sound!"

[Kit shakes head.] "I love those trains. I'll bet yours even puffs smoke."

"Sure does.

"So, what about the math problem?"

"It's stupid! The trains will probably crash into each other before the engineers can stop 'em."

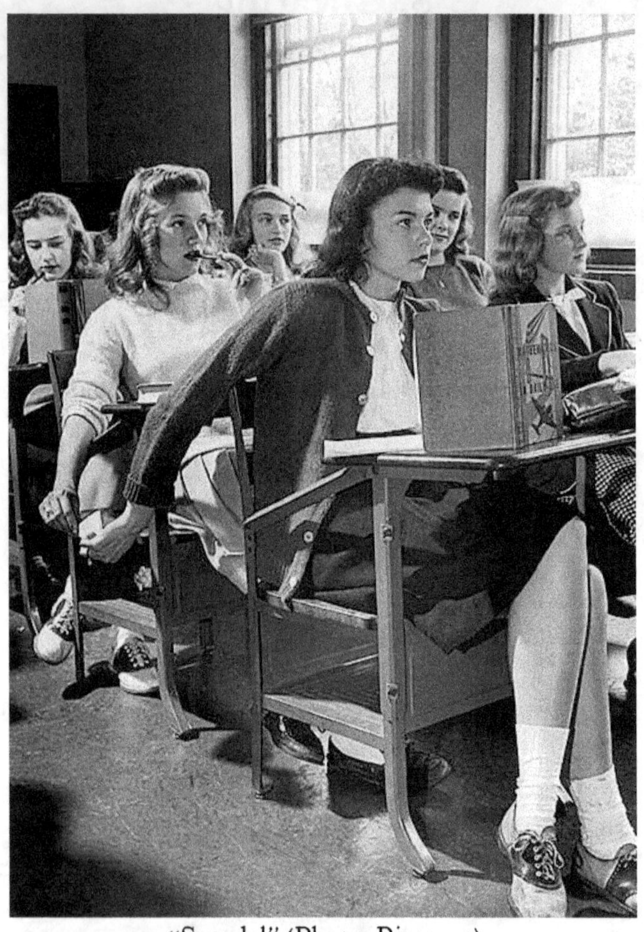

"Scandal" (Photo: Pinterest)

"Psst! Laurie! Can you hear me?"

9. Scandal

Alyssa Devine

"Psst! Laurie! Can you hear me?" she asked, whispering.

"Keep it down, Alison. Miss Patti will hear you."

"No, she won't. She's busy at the board with that algebra problem. Here, take this note. You won't believe what it says!"

Laurie carefully extracts the note from Alison's backward-extended hand, all the time keeping a wary eye on the front of their classroom. Once in her hands and unfolded, she is shocked by its contents.

"Where did you get this?" she whispers.

"Rachel was over at Carole's house last night and asked to use the phone to call her mother. So, she went into the kitchen to use the wall phone, you know—"

"Right. They have that white phone at the end of the counter, near the back door—"

"Exactly. Anyway, she saw this note on a pad next to the phone, and when no one was looking, she copied it."

Laurie shakes her head in disbelief. "I can't believe anyone would do this. It's just horrible."

"I know. What a terrible cake recipe! With that mix, you don't cream shortening, and you certainly don't beat eggs!"

"Youth" (Photo: Pinterest)

"You still smokin' that pipe?"

10. Youth

Theodore Jerome Cohen

"You still smokin' that pipe?"

"Whadda you think? Aren't *you?*"

"Hell, yes, but this sure ain't Prince Albert I'm smoking now!" She laughed and slapped her knee, as if she had told her old friend from childhood something she didn't already know.

"Shhhh, someone'll hear you, and the whole home will be scandalized. You and I already have the worst reputations around here."

"You think I care? When did we *ever* care? Do you remember the stuff we used to pull in high school? We got so many detentions I was sure we'd never graduate."

"Oh, hell, that old Mr. Lane, the principal, had a sweet spot in his heart for you; he'd never have stopped you from graduating. Frankly, I think he couldn't wait to get rid of us, 'specially after that time we snuck out of Miss Henry's trig class to have a smoke in the lavatory and set off all the fire alarms on the third floor."

[The two women cackled while lighting their pipes.]

"And you remember that summer night we went skinny dipping in the Milwaukee River near the North Avenue Bridge?"

"You mean near that place—what was it?"

"Bechstein's Shoot-the-Chutes."

"Yeah, that's it. Haha . . . the boys never could come out of the water until after we left because we took their clothes and threw them into the trees.

"Kids today don't know what they're missin'!"

"Screwed!" (Photo: Wayhome Studio, Big Stock Photo)

"So, dude, like, I thought I was so screwed yesterday!"

11. Screwed!

Theodore Jerome Cohen

"**So,** dude, like, I thought I was so screwed yesterday!"

"Why, what happened, Jalaal?"

"I was sitting in English Lit—"

"You mean Professor Ostenso's class? You poor guy!"

"Tell me! We've been reading Milton's *Paradise Lost*, and the old man's lectures are unbelievable boring! Anyway, so I'm sitting there, pretending like I'm busy scribbling down notes on what he's saying—"

"But you're not, of course, because you're a screw-off!"

[Both men laugh.]

"Right! I'm working on my novel—you know, the one I started earlier this semester. I'd already filled about a third of the notebook with the first five chapters, some character backgrounds, scene descriptions I have in mind, and the like—"

"Why aren't you typing them into your computer?"

"It's not always easy to sit on the bus and type, and sometimes, I don't have my computer available when I get an idea or my muse strikes. So, I just keep my notebook handy."

"Okay, what happened?"

"Well, I'm busy writing when all of a sudden, the guy's standing over me. Busted! And I mean, BUSTED! He doesn't say a word, puts out his hand for the notebook—which I gave him, of course—and I figured I'd never see it again."

"Jesus, after all that work. So, what happened?"

"Well, today he hands it back, and there's a yellow stickie on the top page."

"What did it say?"

" 'Finish the book. I want to know how it ends!' "

"Feel Better Soon" (Photo: lisafx, Big Stock Photo)

"I can't thank you enough for helping me with my books."

12. Feel Better Soon

Theodore Jerome Cohen

"I can't thank you enough for helping me with my books. If you hadn't seen me struggling in the hallway, I'm not sure I would've been able to make it to the library."

The girl released her right forearm crutch, leaned it against the wheelchair, and brushed some stray hairs behind her ear.

"That's okay," responded the boy. "You had your hands full, that's for sure.

"By the way, my name's Jon. Jon Peters. What's yours?"

"Emily Thompson. Yeah, these crutches can be difficult. I sprained both of my ankles in a skating accident over the weekend. I was doing a Lutz in competition over at the coliseum and—"

"And things didn't go according to plan," he said, completing her sentence with a sympathetic smile on his face.

"That's an understatement," she responded.

"And you? How come you're in a wheelchair?"

"Oh, that! Well, it's the usual story, you know," he said cavalierly, chuckling as if he were about to reveal something as ordinary as, say, a broken hip. "I'm paralyzed from the waist down. Swimming accident last summer. The water over at Kingstone's Quarry isn't *quite* as deep as I thought it was.

The color drained from Emily's face. "Oh, you poor thing." She placed her hand on his shoulder, not knowing what else to say or do.

Jon placed his hand on top of hers and looked up at her. "Thanks, but I'll be all right. I just hope you get better soon."

"It's All Relative" (Photo: RMY Auctions; public domain)
Albert Einstein, Princeton, New Jersey, 1933

"So, whaddaya think, Professor?"

13. It's All Relative
Theodore Jerome Cohen

"**So,** whaddaya think, Professor?"

"Vat do you mean, 'Vat do I tink?' "

"I want to know some of your latest thoughts on relativity."

"Vas dat a general qvestion, or did you haf sometink special in mind?"

"You mean, was I inquiring about your first paper—in 1905—about Special Relativity or about your paper ten years later on General Relativity?"

"It makes no diff'rence to me, *mein Freund*, vitch vun we talk about. Vitchever vun you insist upon ist fine vhit me."

"Well, it's not that I'm insisting on anything, Professor Einstein. Makes no difference to me *what* we talk about. I was just trying to make a little light conversation."

"Ah, now ve are talking, my boy. Light! Dat is a subject I *luf* to talk about."

"Okay, so tell me, Professor, do you consider light to be waves or particles?"

"Vell, dat all depends on da situation. If it suits my purposes, it's a vave. If I need it to be tiny packets—as I did for the Special Theory of Relativity—den I insist on it being particles.

"It's all relative, my boy!"

"Storytime" (Photo: Pinterest)

"Don't keep me in suspense! What happens next?"

14. Storytime
Alyssa Devine

"**So?** Don't keep me in suspense! What happens next?"

"You're such a silly goose, Rashi! I read this book to you last month. I thought elephants have such great memories. Don't tell me you've forgotten already."

"I didn't forget. I remember every word, Allison. If I didn't see that book for a year, I could recite it for you, word for word, just as if I had the book in front of me."

"Then why are you insisting I read the book to you again? We could choose a different book. There are many about Babar, you know: *The Story of Babar, The Babar Treasury, Babar the King* . . . we could choose from among these and more. Why do you always insist I read *The Travels of Babar?*"

"Ah, a worthy question, Allison, and one easily answered. First, it's vintage de Brunhoff. This is only the second Babar story, you know. How exciting it is to see them fly off in a balloon, something I shall never be able to do.

"And then, it's scary, too, like when Babar and Celeste are trapped by the circus owner. That's when having you sit with me is such a great comfort. But I know everything will be all right and the Old Lady will help Babar save the day. That just makes me feel good all over again."

"You know what you are, Rashi? You're a big baby! But you're *my* big baby!"

"The Graduate" (Photo: michaeljung, Big Stock Photo)

"Oh, hi, Debra! I guess this must be your dad.
Hi, Mr. Livingstone."

15. The Graduate
Theodore Jerome Cohen

"Oh, hi, Debra! I guess this must be your dad. Hi, Mr. Livingstone, I'm Brian Thompson. It's so nice to meet you."

The young man thrust his right hand forward and vigorously shook the older man's hand.

"No, Brian, you—"

"You must be very proud of her, sir. And not without reason. You know, we were partners in qualitative chemistry during our junior year, and I mean, your daughter was a whiz—a downright WHIZ—when it came to determining what was in a solution. I remember once—"

"Brian—"

"I remember once the professor gave us a solution that contained copper and chlorine ions, and before I even could get our notebook set up, she was off and running. It was just unbelievable, and—"

"BRIAN!"

"Yes, Jennifer?"

"This isn't my dad. My dad's over there with my mother and brother. This is Jeff Fairfield."

"I don't understand. I thought he was your father."

"Well, in a way, he *is* responsible for my being here today. Jeff's the firefighter who rescued me from my crib 21 years ago during our house fire."

"Game Night" (Photo: Pinterest)

"So, whaddaya think? Can we beat 'em?"

16. Game Night

Theodore Jerome Cohen

"**So,** whaddaya think? Can we beat 'em?"

"It ain't gonna be easy, Alicia," said the Number 13—the quarterback for South. "Their quarterback is good . . . I mean, really good! He passed for almost 3600 yards last season. That's about 300 yards per game, so the guy's no slouch, that's for sure."

"Yeah, but we got Jovanovich. That guy can get in there and take down a quarterback better than anyone in our league. He leads the division in sacks. My bet is, if our defense can hold tonight and Jovanovich does his thing, we can force West to abandon their passing game, which is where their strength lies. That should allow you and the offense to dominate!"

"Ha! From your mouth to God's ears. The only thing that worries me is my best pass receiver—Howard—seemed a bit off in practice yesterday. I don't know whether he's still nursing that ankle of his or simply isn't concentrating, but he dropped a number of passes he should have caught with ease."

"I saw that. Give 'im a shot in the 1st quarter, and if you're still uncomfortable, get the coach put Paley into the game. He did a great job last week—you and him seemed to click really well."

"I know. What's up with that? He came out of nowhere in the 4th quarter to save our skin."

"Yeah, it's great to have options."

"So, we still on for the prom? What time should I pick you up?"

"Master Class" (Photo: Fritz Cohen, 1953; public domain)
Jascha Heifetz playing at a concert in Beer-Sheva, Israel

Heifetz had been her idol.

17. Master Class
Theodore Jerome Cohen

Heifetz had been her idol.

She was six when she first saw him perform Tchaikovsky's Violin Concerto in D major with the Chicago Symphony Orchestra. The brilliance of his playing was unlike anything she ever had heard. In her mind, she saw herself on stage, giving life to the composer's masterpiece.

Eleven years later she fulfilled her vision, soloing with the Philadelphia Orchestra. Here, she performed the same composition to a standing-room-only audience that gave her three curtain calls and refused to return to their seats until she agreed to play an encore. At 17 and heralded as one of the world's greatest violin prodigies, she was in demand by the world's orchestras, which lined up to schedule performances.

Almost lost in her memory was an application made years earlier to attend one of Heifetz's master classes. Now, she received word of acceptance. To say she had trepidation is an understatement, but the opportunity to meet Heifetz, much less be tutored by him, was a lifelong dream. For her class she chose the first movement of the Brahms Violin Concerto in D major, which she had recently performed to high acclaim with the London Symphony Orchestra.

"No, no," shouted Heifetz as he stopped her barely 15 seconds into the first movement. "This won't do at all! Where is your passion? And why isn't there more clarity on the notes in the higher register?!" The rest of the session went no better.

She now regrets having ever met the man.

"Code Talkers" (Photo: Smithsonian Institution,
Bureau of American Ethnology (1897 - 1965); public domain)

"And to think it almost didn't happen."

18. Code Talkers

Theodore Jerome Cohen

"And to think it almost didn't happen."

"What are you talking about?"

"I'm talking about the fact that in the late 1800s, the U.S. government and Christian missionaries established boarding schools for American Indian children. The whole idea was to eliminate the Indians' traditional ways of life and bring them into mainstream American culture."

"Well, I assume they fought this movement."

"Of course, but even those who resisted finally relented; in the end, no other schools were available. Once the children were separated from their families, they were not reunited with them for as many as four years. And adding insult to injury, the children were forced to dress as Americans and cut their hair. They had to assume English names, replace their traditional religious practices with Christianity—something that was forcibly imposed on them—and were taught their cultures were basically inferior."

"But again, you started by saying 'it almost didn't happen.' What did you mean?"

"Well, many Navajo children continued to speak their language—which, as you know, is unwritten—among themselves whenever the White Man wasn't around. It's a good thing, too, because a number grew up to serve in the U.S. Marines as the famed Navajo Code Talkers. Even today, there are those who wonder if the U.S. military would have achieved victory in the Pacific had it not been for the Navajos who retained a knowledge of their language."

"Final Exam" (Photo: Reb Beatty, Anne Arundel
Community College)

"What's this?"

19. Final Exam

Theodore Jerome Cohen

"What's this?"

"Oh, that. It's a picture of one of my students taking her final exam in my American history course."

"Really? Is all that stuff in front of her the exam? I know you had a lot to cover—didn't you say you were focusing on World War I, the peace Wilson negotiated, and how it led to the Third Reich?—but that's a bit ridiculous."

"Yeah, you're right. I did put a lot of emphasis on how oppressive the Allies were when it came to Germany after the war. But no, the actual exam is just the one sheet in front of her, and all it contains are ten multiple-choice questions on the front and three short essay questions on the back. Not a difficult exam, if I say so myself, given the students had two hours to complete it."

"So, what are all those notes in front of her? Was it an open-book exam? I mean, it looks like she has a ton of material there."

"Well, I screwed up."

"Whaddaya mean, 'screwed up'?"

"I told the students they could bring a 3-by-5 card to the exam."

"What's wrong with that?"

"I forgot to specify 3-by-5 inches. This student brought notes on a card measuring 3-by-5 *feet*."

"Wow! Well played!"

"Prom Night" (Photo: 9GAG.com)

"So, Eddy, how'd prom night go?"

20. Prom Night
Theodore Jerome Cohen

"So, Eddy, how'd prom night go?"

"Oh, all right, I guess."

"You guess? YOU GUESS?! Kitty McGuire is the prettiest girl in the class and you say 'You guess'?! What the hell's the matter with you? I can think of ten guys who would give their left—"

"Yeah, yeah, I know. And you're looking at me and wondering how a schlub who couldn't even get a date for the last football hop ended up with McGuire, right?"

"Well, the thought crossed my mind. Think about it, she's a goddess. Did you see her at that last football game, when she was standing at the top of the cheerleading pyramid? There wasn't a man in the stands who could take his eyes offa her!

"So, how *did* you land that date? You musta asked her really early, before anyone else could get to her."

"Oh, no, nothin' like that. In fact, I asked her the night before the prom."

"The night before? Are you f---ing kidding me? You mean she didn't have a date by then?"

"Nope. But I sure learned *why* when I picked her up?"

"Whaddaya mean?"

"Well, her grandfather works for the sheriff's department, her dad's on the police force, and her brother is the president of the local NRA chapter."

"Spring Fling" (Photo: Pinterest)

"Hey, Emily, who's the handsome dude?"

21. Spring Fling
Alyssa Devine

"Hey, Emily, who's the handsome dude?"

"Oh, hi, Alyssa. That's Josh Bennett. The picture was taken at my sorority's Spring Fling back in May of '98. Josh had just graduated from West Point and was home on leave before reporting to UH-60 Flight School at Fort Rucker for training as a pilot on Black Hawk helicopters."

"Wow, he looks like a neat guy."

"I'll say. From what his friends told me, both his commanders *and* subordinates at West Point respected and liked him. He was just one of those people who got along with everyone—congenial, enthusiastic, always had a good word to say about others. I loved being with him."

"I can see that! Sooo—"

"Has anyone ever told you you're nosey?"

"Just about everybody."

"Well, he took his training, graduated, and was assigned to a squadron while I continued my education at the University of Wisconsin-Madison. We tried to maintain a relationship, but it was difficult. It wasn't long before he was sent to Kosovo, then moved all over the world for reasons known only to the Army, and, well, you get the picture. Eventually, we lost touch. I still think about him almost every day and treasure this picture more than words can say."

"Then, you have no idea where he is today?"

"Oh, yes . . . Josh is in Arlington National Cemetery. He died in 2003 when his Black Hawk was shot down during the invasion of Baghdad."

See Endnote 4.

"Problem Solved" (Photo: Pinterest)

"I can't help but notice everyone's head is shaved."

22. Problem Solved

Theodore Jerome Cohen

"I want to thank you, Dr. Mohammadian, for inviting me to observe your third-grade class this afternoon."

"Please, Ted, call me Ali," the teacher responded, smiling.

"Okay, Ali. So, what are the students studying at the moment?"

"This morning we're continuing our work in mathematics. We're learning about the meter as a formal unit of length. The students have just measured the width of the classroom and in a minute, we'll see how everyone did. Then, we're going to measure the length, and—"

"And from there, you'll introduce the concept of area."

"Of course," he laughed. "You know, I could sit down and let *you* teach my class. They all speak English, you know . . . well, enough to get by in a simple conversation at least."

"That's wonderful, Ali. But let me ask you a question. I can't help but notice everyone's head is shaved. Is that a requirement imposed by the school board?"

"Oh no, Ted. It came about because we have a student who, having an unknown medical condition, was going bald. The other students were bullying him, so—"

"So, you made everyone shave their heads?"

"Actually, no. *I* shaved my head, and within a few days, the entire class came to school with their heads shaved. More amazing than that, the bullying stopped. Cold!"[2]

---

[2] This story was inspired by real events.

"A Speaking Part" (Photo: Pinterest)

"So, what did you think about the story, Odysseus?"

23. A Speaking Part
Theodore Jerome Cohen

"**So,** what did you think about the story, Odysseus?"

"Wow! Sir Arthur Conan Doyle certainly penned a beautiful piece of literature there, John."

"I agree. It's easy to see why 'The Adventure of Silver Blaze' was one of his favorites. I mean, the entire setting was simply marvelous, with the story set in the moorland of southern Devon. And those late-Victorian sporting scenes were outta this world. It almost makes me wish I had lived during those times."

"Me, too. We could've had such fun together, tramping over the English countryside, attending the horse races—"

"Speaking of horse races, how'd you like the way Conan Doyle worked them into this story, with the disappearance of that famous racehorse Silver Blaze and the murder of its trainer?"

"Well, that was outstanding. I couldn't wait for us to get to the park so we could finish the story!"

"I know. I've never seen you so eager to go for your walk. Anyway, tell me: what was your favorite part?"

"I loved it that Conan Doyle let the dog be the key to Sherlock Holmes' solving the crime. But next time, maybe he could give him a speaking part."

"Oorah!" (Photo: Pinterest)

"They assigned me to a class with the toughest students in the entire school."

24. Oorah!

Theodore Jerome Cohen

"They *what?!*"

"Right off the bat, on the very first day of school, they assigned me to a class with the toughest students in the entire school."

"But they understood you were new to teaching, right . . . that you had just retired from the Marine Corps?"

"Oh, yeah. But they'd had so much trouble with these kids that the principal had run out of options. The last teacher he had assigned to that class almost had a nervous breakdown and was on medical leave."

"Geez, they musta been terrors. The principal was aware you had injured your back during the summer, right, and that you were wearing a plaster cast around the entire upper part of your body?"

"Oh, yeah, he knew. Fortunately, my shirt and suitcoat covered it up completely. Besides, I wasn't in any pain. So, I just sucked it up and thought, 'What the hell, why not?!' I knew the punks would test me from the get-go, and sure enough, there was bedlam from the moment I stepped into the classroom."

"So, what did you do?"

"Well, I opened a window as wide as I could, sat down, and when a strong breeze started to make my tie flap, I stapled the damn thing to my chest.

"I never had another problem."

"Fraternity Prank" (Photo: Pinterest)

"What's the problem *this* time, officer?"

25. Fraternity Prank
Theodore Jerome Cohen

"What's the problem *this* time, officer?"

"What's the problem? *What's the problem?!* Can't you see what the goddam problem is?! Those a--holes in Delta Tau Chi got this guy drunk—my guess is he's a pledge—and then, they hoisted him upside-down to sleep it off. According to the people across the street, he's been here all night. I am *soooo* sick of this s--t!"

"I know what you mean."

"No, you can't possibly *begin* to understand the pain these people cause me. I no sooner came on duty this morning—Sunday morning!—and Dispatch sent me on this call. Last Sunday, same story. That time it was about a horse someone led into the dean's office, where it died. Talk about a mess! And the stench? These people are *animals!*"

"Hasn't the university taken action?"

"Faber College? They've tried to curb the excesses, but the fraternity members couldn't care less. They just do whatever they want. Ride motorcycles in the house? Sure, why not? Drive over the lawn? Makes sense to them.

"I'll tell you what, they scare the hell outta me. Every week things keep escalating. And with homecoming a month off, I shudder to think what might happen."

"Sounds like a good plot for a movie to me."

"Sure . . . like someone's gonna make a film about those losers!"

See Endnote 5.

"Virtue" (Photo: monkeybusinessimages, Big Stock Photo)

"Please have a seat. I want to talk with you about Jalissa."

26. Virtue

Theodore Jerome Cohen

"You asked me to stop by after school hours, Mr. Lane?"

"Oh, yes, Mr. Washington. Thanks for coming in. Please have a seat. I want to talk with you about Jalissa."

"Gosh, I hope she hasn't done anything wrong. She's been so happy here at Penn Central Elementary. I know it's been a bit of an adjustment for her from the inner city and all, but she's really put her mind to her studies, and if I remember correctly, didn't she end up with all A's at the end of the last reporting period?"

"Yes, her grades are good . . . excellent, in fact. No, it's not her academics that I want to talk about. It's something that happened in the cafeteria earlier this week—something I thought you should know about."

"Oh, gracious, I was afraid this would happen sooner or later. My wife LaKeishha and I figured that sooner or later there was going to be trouble. Tell me, how bad was it?"

The principal laughed. "That's not it at all, Mr. Washington."

"It isn't?"

"No, sir. I want to tell you how proud we all are of your daughter. The people in the cafeteria told me that your daughter paid for the person behind her in line on Monday. When they asked her why, she said she was paying it forward, just like her dad sometimes does when they're driving on the turnpike."

"Sister Marie" (Photo: Pinterest)

"Do you remember that day?"

27. Sister Marie

Theodore Jerome Cohen

"**Do** you remember that day?"

"Are you kidding?! That was taken on St. Patrick's Day, 1948, one of the few times I wasn't in trouble with Sister Marie."

"I'll say. Boy, did she ever have it in for *you*! Not that you didn't deserve it."

"Hey, I thought you were my friend."

"I was, but believe me—I mean, take a look at the size of that woman—when she turned around from the blackboard and caught you dipping Gwendolyn's hair into your inkwell, I knew better than get in 'er way."

"Ah yes, Gwendolyn, who loved to swish her blond pigtails back and forth in front of me. I thought I'd teach her a lesson by sticking 'em in ink."

"And a fine job you did, Timothy O'Leary . . . a fine job, indeed. If I recall correctly, it was a week before the welts on your wrist subsided after Sister Marie took her ruler to your hand."

"Ha! That hurt, all right. Jesus, I had all I could do not to cry—that would have been the greater sin, to my mind. Just seeing Gwendolyn and the others starin' at me was bad enough. But cry? Not me. I just thank God Sister Marie never told my Father, bless his soul, or I probably wouldn't have been able to sit down ever again."

"Well, here's to the good Sister: 'May the sun shine warm upon your face. And rains fall soft upon your fields.' "

"Graduation" (Photo: Pinterest)

"Julie, have I shown you my husband's graduation picture?"

28. Graduation

Theodore Jerome Cohen

"Julie, have I shown you my husband's graduation picture?"

"No, Elise, do you have it on your cell phone?"

"Now that's a silly question," Elise responded, pulling the phone from her purse. "What kind of wife would I be if I didn't have a million pictures here of our family, the children, and most of all, the grandchildren?!"

"I know, I know . . . the small pleasures in life. But that truly was a special occasion."

"Oh, yes, it's been a long slog for Brad, that's for sure. He had to go to work in his senior year of college to help his mother after his father died. And then, just as things were starting to go well, there was that terrible car accident—the one that took his sight. Frankly, it's a miracle he lived. The only good thing that came from it—other than, thank God, he lived—was the settlement from the insurance company, which finally allowed him to pursue his dream: a master's degree. And there he is—isn't that a terrific picture?—right after receiving his MBA. I'm sooo proud of him. And he even has a job waiting for him with a major tax firm."

"I'm so happy for you both! And how cute that his dog has a graduation gown on."

"Oh, that's not just for show. The college awarded Chauncey an honorary master's degree for sitting through every one of Brad's classes."

"Sister Ethel" (Photo: Pinterest)

"Hey, Joe, have you been following the debate
about arming teachers?"

29. Sister Ethel

Theodore Jerome Cohen

"Hey, Joe, have you been following the debate about arming teachers?"

"Are you kidding? I can't turn the TV on these days without seeing something about that!"

"So, whaddaya think?"

"I think it's the dumbest ideas to come down the pike since the release of the dollar coin. Teachers didn't sign up to play cops—they're there to *teach.* And God knows, they're already burdened with more than enough to do in the classroom, given what most of 'em are paid. Hell, according to my daughter, half the kids in her child's second-grade class show up every morning without even having had breakfast, and the other half can't remember what they learned yesterday. Talk about frustration!"

"I'm with you on that. Our son and his wife had to help our grandson's third-grade teacher this year by giving her money to purchase supplies. The school's budget doesn't even have enough money in it to cover the paper and crayons she needs for her art sessions."

"And people want to arm teachers? Gimme a break! What are they gonna do? Turn our schools into armed fortresses?!"

"Well, it certainly was different when we attended St. Catherine's, wasn't it?"

"You bet! No one—and I mean *no one*—ever messed with Sister Ethel."

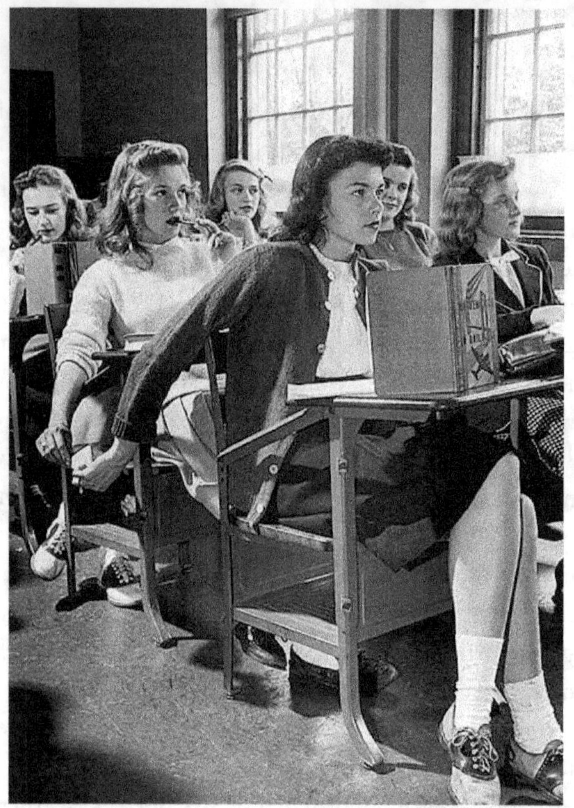

"High School Reunion" (Photo: Pinterest)

"Welcome home," I shouted to my wife, Marsha, as she alighted from a rail passenger car at the Trenton train station upon returning from her 30th high school reunion in New York City."

30. High School Reunion
Theodore Jerome Cohen

"Welcome home," I shouted to my wife, Marsha, as she alighted from a rail passenger car at the Trenton train station upon returning from her 30th high school reunion in New York City. "So, how'd it go?"

"Oh, it went fine," she responded with an air of finality and a broad smile on her face. "Just fine!" She pecked me on the cheek, handed me her overnight bag, and, after switching her crossbody handbag from her right to her left side, followed me to the parking garage.

Whaddaya know?! I thought. I was surprised. Truth be told, I'd been reluctant to ask, given the circumstances surrounding her trip. I'd watched through the years as first, an invitation for her 10th reunion arrived in the mail, and then, one for her 20th. Both were met with the same pursed lips and scowl. Within a minute, each invitation was torn in half, quartered, and dispatched to the trash. Obviously, my expectations for the half-life of the invitation to her 30th had not been good. Yet here she was, back from the event, mind intact and a smile on her face. Life is full of surprises!

The ride to Washington Crossing, our home since we graduated from college, was spent mostly in silence, punctuated now and then by comments she made regarding the compositions aired on the local classical music station.

"Well, at least it must've been nice to see some of your old classmates after all this time," I finally opined. "I know *I'd* be curious about some of the guys I went to school with, that's for sure."

Silence. We were in different worlds. But she did seem at peace with herself.

It's not as if she never spoke about high school. Occasionally, while we were dating—we met when she was a freshman in college, and I was a sophomore— she would talk about growing up on Manhattan's Upper East Side and attending a private high school located not far from her apartment building on Lexington Avenue. She had a good friend—as I recall, her name was Julie—

who lived nearby. I specifically remember they shared the same birth date and were once inseparable. They took all the same classes, double dated, dined and attended the theater with their parents together—things like that. They spent summers at a camp in Maine, too, where they were teammates, counselors-in-training, and then, counselors. They apparently were the kind of kids that, if you didn't know better, you'd think were fraternal twins. And yes, she once mentioned they often completed each other's sentences.

So, I was perplexed when both the 10th and 20th reunions passed without the slightest hint of interest on Marsha's part. *Not even an interest in seeing Julie again?* I thought at the time, not that I brought it up.

Friends come and go. God knows that's the truth. I hadn't seen any of *my* high school classmates since leaving the Midwest 30 years earlier. With the exception of two men, I don't even correspond with any of my former classmates, and those two I met at college. Life moves on—the Army, jobs, kids. High school? That's ancient history.

It's not like she didn't talk about those days, though. Often, on our autumn walks along the Delaware—at the spot where Washington crossed that great river on Christmas Night in 1776—she would recite portions of Helen Hunt Jackson's 'October's Bright Blue Weather' or of Molière's *Don Juan*, both of which she learned in two of her favorite high school classes, English and Drama. The fact is, she *loved* high school, which made her attitude toward class reunions all the more puzzling.

It came as a surprise to me, then, how she responded when the invitation for the 30th reunion arrived. Instead of the expected grimaces and conspicuous destruction of the formal announcement, Marsha promptly sat, completed the enclosed form, made her dinner selection, penned a check, and marched to the mailbox at the end of our driveway, where she deposited the return envelope in the mailbox for the next day's pickup.

"Well, that's a change," I noted, setting aside *The Philadelphia Enquirer* and taking a sip of my coffee. "Frankly, I'm thrilled to see you taking advantage of the opportunity to rekindle some old friendships. I'll bet it'll be fun to see your former classmates and learn what's happened to them over the years, especially in the case of your friend Julie. Gosh, you two were like sisters."

"Julie's dead!" she snapped, nearly biting my head off. "She died two years ago—ovarian cancer. Her mother told my mother at one of their card games. Mom called me."

"I'm sorry, darling."

"Well, I am, too. But it's over. And now, it's time to put the record straight."

Put the record straight? What the hell is she talking about? I said nothing, letting her words hang in the air. If this conversation were to continue, it would have to be on *her* terms. For my part, I had no idea how to defuse the land mine I'd stepped on!

We sat in silence for several seconds before she spoke.

"It started near the end of our senior year, and always on a Monday morning. Julie would arrive late, well after first period, and use the same excuse: she had to either stay home to help her mother—who she said had leukemia— or take her mother for an early morning doctor's appointment. This garnered all kinds of sympathy from the school administrators and teachers who, of course, took her at her word. No one dared contact her parents, fearing a call might bring her terminally ill mother to the phone. We, her classmates, were horrified by the news and gave her all the support and sympathy we could.

"Over time, her tardiness turned into day-long absences, something, she said, had to do with her having to stay at the hospital with her mother while she underwent chemotherapy. Again, all of this was excused by the school without the slightest request for a note from home."

"Did you ask her what type of leukemia she had? There are several types, you know."

Marsha laughed. "You're kidding me, right? I was a high school senior. What did I know about leukemia?!

"Anyway, it didn't take long before I began to suspect her story. It didn't make sense. For one thing, I ate dinner at Julie's several times each month— they lived in the apartment building across the street from ours, you know— and I used to, like, nonchalantly but carefully look at her mother when we were talking at the table. I never once saw *anything* that told me she was ill. Not once! The woman always seemed so vibrant, talking about the latest Broadway play she had seen or an exhibit she had taken in at the Metropolitan Museum of Art. She never uttered a word about being sick or having seen a doctor. Nothing! And besides, she had a full head of hair; beautiful, silky blonde hair that fell well below her shoulders. Chemotherapy, my foot!

"I also told my mother what Julie had said. She was aghast. She couldn't believe it. Aside from a cold Julie's mother had had earlier in the year, mom said the woman was as healthy as a horse. And mom would've known; they were bridge partners, played every week—twice, not counting the tournaments they entered.

"Meanwhile, I guess my skepticism started showing."

"Whaddaya mean?"

"I began to give Julie the cold shoulder. Basically, I began ignoring her."

"And?"

"And, the other girls turned on me; said I was a bitch; told me I had no empathy and wasn't the kind of friend Julie needed now, when her mother was dying."

"That musta been rough."

"They were unbelievably cruel. They excluded me from all their activities just at the time when our senior year was coming to a close. For that, I never forgave them."

"And Julie?"

"Ah, yes . . . dear Julie. The straw that broke the camel's back was the day my mother took me downtown for an early Monday morning appointment to have my teeth cleaned. We no sooner had left the dentist's office when I saw Julie and her college boyfriend hail a cab in front of a hotel on the other side of 3rd Avenue. Now I'm starting to think. What if they'd spent the night there? So much for taking care of her mom on Monday mornings!

"I confronted her later that day between classes and told her what I'd seen. She broke down and admitted it was all a hoax, that there was nothing wrong with her mother! The unmitigated gall of that woman! I was furious!"

The fire in my wife's eyes at that moment was unlike anything I'd ever seen. "Sounds like mental illness to me, perhaps a form of Munchausen syndrome by proxy, except her mother wasn't even aware of the fact her daughter was asserting she had leukemia. Just an extreme attempt to get sympathy and special attention, or—"

"Or what?!" Marsha snapped.

"Or she simply wanted to spend as much time as possible with her boyfriend before he went home for the summer and didn't give a flying fig about anyone or anything else, including you, her best friend."

"You got that right! And because of that, her friends turned the last semester of my senior year into a living Hell! Which is where I told Julie she could go. And that was the end of that.

"Now, the rest of the class will learn the truth about Julie. And if they don't believe me, they can ask her mother, who's not only alive and well, but who still plays a brilliant game of contract bridge twice a week with my mother on the Upper East Side."

"Molly" (Photo: michelangeloop, Big Stock Photo)

"I seem to remember a certain, special young woman. What was her name?"
"Ah, you must be talking about Molly . . . Molly Patterson."

31. Molly
Theodore Jerome Cohen

"**S**teve? Steve Jennings?"

"Dan Rollins! Well, I'll be go to hell! Is that really you? My god, what's it been, 50 years?"

The two men shook hands, then embraced in a bear hug before sitting at the bar in Madison's Edgewater Hotel, not far from the state capitol.

"What's your poison?" asked Rollins, signaling to the bartender, who already was making his way toward them."

"Oh, the usual . . . Jack Daniel's on the rocks. Smooth as it comes."

"Make that two," said Rollins to the bartender, who had overheard the conversation and proceeded to set two napkins and a dish of peanuts in front of the men.

"You got it, Mr. Rollins," replied the bartender, who obviously knew his customer.

"So, Steve" continued Dan," what brings you back to the scene of our youthful indiscretions?"

"Well, it *has* been 50 years since we graduated. So, when the class of '66 reached out and issued invitations for the 50th reunion, I thought, what the hell, it might be great to see some of the old haunts again. You know, Bascom Hill, the Brathaus, Rennebohm's drug *store* . . . places like that. But I never expected to see you here."

"Oh, heck, I never left," replied Dan. "Just stayed put and continued working for the real estate firm that employed me part-time when I was in college. I ended up buying the company in 1983, Made quite a good living for Judy and me, too, and—"

"Hey, that's right. I remember you were dating Judy all through our junior and senior years. Man, you were a lucky guy. She always reminded me of Natalie Wood. How *is* she?"

"Judy passed away three years ago, Steve. Ovarian cancer. It had already progressed to stage IV when they detected it. By then, it was too late; there was nothing they could do. She died a month later."

"I'm so sorry, Dan," said Steve, shaking his head. "That must've been difficult."

They sat in silence for several seconds, broken only by the bartender arriving with their drinks.

"Here you go, gents. How we doin' on the peanuts?"

"We're good, Joe" replied Dan, giving him a weak smile.

The men picked up their drinks and before Dan could speak, Steve toasted: "To Judy."

"To Judy," Dan replied.

The men sipped their whiskeys.

"Anyway," continued Dan, "you wouldn't recognize our little city today, that's for sure."

"I'll say. I took a quick tour around the campus and Fraternity Row on my way from the airport, Frankly, I had a tough time making my way around the area. You can't drive on State Street anymore. What's up with that?"

"Isn't that a hoot?" Dan replied. "City vehicles, pedestrians, and bikes only."

"I also tried to find the house we used to live in on North Francis. Remember? We had that little apartment on the third floor. It didn't even have a shower; that was to be found on the second floor and was used by everybody in the building."

"You bet. That was the house next to the church of Holy Rollers. Remember how they used to 'rock out' during Sunday night services?"

"Do I! Well, I can tell you this, the old house is gone. So much for *those* good memories."

"So, what about you?" asked Dan, sipping his whiskey. "Last I heard, you'd been commissioned as a second lieutenant in the Army and were off to the war. At that point, you evaporated into thin air."

"Yeah, sorry about that. Things got a little hectic once I went on active duty. The war in Nam was heating up, as you recall, and within two days of being commissioned, the Army shipped my ass to Ft. Gordon for two months of post-ROTC Signal Officer training. From there I got assigned to support to the comm center at Tan Son Nhut Air Base. Man, did we take a shellacking in December of that year. You're lucky you were 4F, my friend. That was no party over there."

"Sorry, buddy. Would have been right there with you if it hadn't been for my ticker," Dan replied sheepishly.

Steve, sipping his drink, waved his hand as if to say *forget it.* Then he grabbed a handful of peanuts, popped them into his mouth, and continued. "Anyway, I put in three tours in Nam over ten years. By the end of February, 1975, I'd made lieutenant colonel and was assigned as the chief signal officer in the US Embassy in Saigon."

"The end of February?" Dan couldn't believe his ears. "Are you freakin' kidding me? Then you musta been there when the city fell that April?"

"Of course I was there. Shit! I was *in* the goddamn embassy as the Viet Cong were moving on the compound. That could be me you see in some photos, helping people climb into those Huey's that were touching down on the roof long enough for us to load them up and get 'em on their way out to sea."

"Jesus!"

"Well, there wasn't much more I could do. I mean, I'd already torched all of the classified documents and destroyed the comm center's communications and crypto equipment. Might as well help out on the roof before getting out of Dodge. The embassy was supposed to have been the secondary evacuation point for embassy personnel, but in the end, it was overwhelmed with desperate South Vietnamese. I barely made it out with the shirt on my back. Hundreds were left behind.

"I finally ended up on the *USS Midway.* There were so many Hueys inbound, flown by both US and RVN pilots, that as soon as one landed, the ship's crew pushed it overboard to make way for the next. What a disaster. It finally got so bad we were radioing pilots to drop off passengers and then, take off and ditch at sea. We had boats waiting to rescue the pilots, of course. I had nightmares for years after that."

Steve shook his head and took another sip from his glass.

"Wow," remarked Dan, "that's quite a story. Thank you for your service, old friend! Who would have thought you had it in you, given all the stuff you pulled in your college days."

"What do you mean 'all the stuff I pulled in my college days'?" Steve responded, laughing.

"Just saying," said Dan, with a wry grin on his face. "I seem to remember a certain, special young woman— What was her name?"

"Ah, you must be talking about Molly . . . Molly Patterson."

"Yes, that's the lass. I remember how, all too often, I would come back to our apartment after lunch, only to find your shoes outside the door, letting me know you and Molly were, shall we say, enjoying an afternoon delight and I should cool my heels elsewhere."

Steve laughed. "Actually, I put the shoes out there hoping the building's valet would shine them. But I have to tell you, I'd take an afternoon with Molly over a three-hour electronics lab any day of the week."

"Well, by my reckoning, you did. Frequently. Fact is, I don't know how you ever made the grades you did while you two were dating. So, did you ever make an honest woman of her?"

"Sadly, no. And you know, Dan, even after all those years together, I still can't figure out what happened. We went steady from the time we were sophomores, we both loved children, and I figured we'd get married at some point. We talked about it . . . she knew that the life of an Army officer's wife might not be the easiest, with long separations, frequent moves, and all that. But we were in love, and we figured we could make it work.

"Then, after graduation, she went back to New York, and I went on active duty. We corresponded for a while, but it wasn't long before she stopped writing. I don't know if she met someone, whether her parents put the kibosh on our relationship—I always got the feeling they weren't keen on me, my being from the Midwest and all—if the Army was a put-off, or what. But it got to the point where she simply stopped writing, and I figured it was time to move on."

Dan signaled the bartender for another round. Upon its arrival he proposed a toast: "To Molly."

"To Molly," responded Steve. "I hope she's happy somewhere."

"You Can't Go Home" (Photo: RTimages, Big Stock Photo)

"He told himself it should have felt like a homecoming."

32. You Can't Go Home

Theodore Jerome Cohen

He told himself it should have felt like a homecoming, landing in what he once, but no more, considered his hometown. Yet, to Don Loman, now an aging representative for a tool and die manufacturer based in Kansas City, Missouri, his return to Milwaukee aboard a Midwest Express 737 early one spring day in 2006 seemed like just another business trip, one of literally thousands he had made throughout the United States while working for various firms in the field since being discharged from the Navy in the mid-1970s.

Don was in the Cream City for a convention, not to work, per se, but for an annual industry conference sponsored by a large industrial association. Importantly, the conference also was intended to feature exhibits of association's members' latest products in the fields of computer-aided design, machining, and manufacturing; plating; and the like. While Loman's company was a bit-player in field, it still was important that manufacturers knew its manufacturing capabilities had stayed current with the needs of their customers.

As the plane approached the city from the south and settled onto runway at Milwaukee's Mitchell International Airport, the pilot raised the wing spoilers, slowing the aircraft abruptly and jolting Don back to his childhood on the north side of the city in the 1950s and '60s. Then, he woke every weekday morning to long blasts from the 7:00 a.m. whistles atop the plants across the city signaling the start of the day shifts. He recalled having a good life, one full of friends, summers free to ride around the neighborhood and beyond on his large Schwinn bike, or simply having the time to while away an entire day on the city's mass transportation system after paying a dime and using transfers, some of which he found on the street, to change from one streetcar or trolley bus to another. "No one bothered me," he'd tell his mom. "No one even spoke to me. Don't worry so much."

High school—he attended what once was known as East Division—was challenging but fun. He recalled excelling at both math and science, and recalled attending the big shows in the school's auditorium presented by DuPont and other corporations, some with rather spectacular finales.

Today, sadly, those memories were bitter sweet. While a scholarship to Milwaukee's Marquette University seemingly had put him on a path toward a BS in Physics, the threat of being drafted into the Army at the end of his sophomore year sent him running for the North Shore's interurban station for a quick trip south to Naval Station Great Lakes, somewhat north of Chicago. There, he enlisted in the Navy. Within months, he found himself aboard an aircraft carrier from which aircraft were launched to bomb North Vietnam, support US and RVN combat operations, and medevac wounded personnel.

Three tours of duty later, suffering from drug addiction and PTSD, he was flown to San Francisco for discharge. Being spit on by passengers at that city's international air terminal seemed a fitting end, at least to him, to a war he had come to question, both for what it had done to him and to the people of Vietnam.

But where to go? He couldn't go back to Milwaukee. There was nothing there for him now. His parents had died in an automobile accident on the interstate between Chicago and Milwaukee several years earlier while he was in Southeast Asia. At the time, he wasn't even able to return Stateside in time for their funeral services. Fact is, they were buried in Colorado Springs, which had been the family's home before his father moved them to Milwaukee after he accepted an offer from one of the largest industrial manufacturers on the city's South Side.

So, Don flew to Colorado Springs, went to the cemetery, and paid his respects, following which he checked in the VA for rehabilitation. It was a year before he was ready to find work. Fortunately, the times were good, and given his love of math and physics, it wasn't long before he found an entry position as a manufacturer's rep for a firm in the space field.

Now, several job iterations and decades later, here he was again, in Milwaukee, walking through that city's air terminal, on his way to pick up a rental car before heading to his hotel near the city's arena. Once registered and unpacked, his plan was to slip into the arena and tour the exhibition hall while the association's members assembled their booths and displays for the convention's opening on the following day.

———◆———

"Don?! Don Loman?! Is that you?"

Don barely had time to turn around when a man grabbed his left shoulder and spun him around on the convention's exhibit floor.

"I knew it was you!" cried an excited Jim Reynolds.

Don immediately recognized the man. "Well, what the— How many years has it been, Jim?"

"Gosh, it has to be at least 40 if it's a day! How the hell are you, my friend?"

Both men had been in the same high school graduating class, and in fact, had gone through the four years in the same homeroom. They were geeks, in every sense of the word, taking all the same classes, focusing more on academics than girls—they were the ones usually serving cokes and chips at the school's proms while the in-crowd danced—and, in general, more interested in an upcoming math competition than finding a date for Saturday night.

"This is unbelievable," enthused Jim. "Why, just the other night, I was thinking about that Saturday when your dad drove the Math Club to Mount Mary University for the All-Milwaukee Math Competition. Do you remember that? Remember how Mr. Peters threw test questions at us for a month before the competition after school . . . God, I was seeing trigonometric equations in my sleep!"

"In know. But I loved every minute of it. Some of those questions were real ball-busters. I think Jane Fields—remember, she came in first on our team— beat me out by one point. But you did pretty well yourself, as I recall."

"Right behind you, buddy boy! And even though our school came in second, I was walking on air."

"Me, too," echoed Don. "That was a great day! By the way, I wonder what ever happened to Mr. Peters."

"I haven't the faintest. Anyway, what brings you to the show, Jim. Do you work in the field? I rep a small tool and die company outta Kansas City, Missouri."

83

"Naw, nothing like that. I'm in real estate. But remember how we used to love mechanical drawing . . . how we'd stay after school to ink our work. That always stuck with me. Years later I built a small machine shop in my basement. Nothin' fancy, you know: a milling machine, lathe, drill press. Stuff like that. I love working on engines, gun sights, whatever comes along. It's tinkering, but the fact is, not many people do that anymore. It's just a part of me; been with me all my life."

"That's terrific. I'd love to see the shop sometime."

"Tell you what; I'll pick you up at noon tomorrow, spin around to my place—I'm only 20 minutes from here—I'll fix some sandwiches, and I'll show it to you. I'll have you back on the convention floor in no time."

Don stuck out his hand. "Done. I'll meet in front of your hotel lobby at noon."

—◆◦◆—

True to his word, Jim was there, waiting, at noon. Don hopped in on the passenger side, and the pair sped off to Jim's home in Brookfield, a suburb west of the city. The traffic lights favored their trip, and they arrived in less than 20 minutes. After a quick lunch, they went down into the home's basement.

Well, whaddaya think?" asked Jim, when they had finished going through the array of machines and tools arrayed before them.

Don let out a breathy, whistling sound. "This is some workshop, all right. I'm in the business, and I'll tell you this, you have the capability to produce some fine products given what I've seen. The boresight you made for your friend's rifle is a thing of beauty, if I ever seen one. That should be entered into competition."

Jim laughed. "It was. Last year. And it won first place. See. Here's the blue ribbon and the photo of me accepting the award."

"Can't beat that!" said Don.

"Say, I have an idea. Remember how we were talking yesterday about the math competition and Mr. Peters. He always was my favorite," said Jim.

"Mine, too," replied Don.

"What say we play hooky this afternoon, run over to the high school, see if they have a current address for him, and then run over to his house and say 'Hello'."

"That's a great idea."

It took a half-hour to reach the school, find a parking place and enter the building. Neither man had been there since the day they graduated. The changes they encountered were shocking.

Their entry was blocked by a locked door. Only after announcing themselves was the door electronically unlocked by the attendant, whereupon they were required to sign in, put on badges, and walk to the receptionist's desk under the watchful eye of the school's resource officer.

"Man, things sure have changed from when we were here," mumbled Don as the men approached the receptionist.

"Good afternoon, gentlemen. How may I help you?"

"Yes, ma'am. My name is Jim Reynolds. My friend is Don Lohman. We graduated from here a few years ago—well, perhaps more than a few."

The receptionist chuckled. "It's been more than a few years for all of us, that's for sure."

"In any event, Don's in town for a trade show, and we thought we'd stop in a see our old high school after all these years."

"Well, the school's changed, that's for sure," she responded, "greatly expanded, for one thing, to accommodate a much larger student population. You should visit the new media center, one of the finest of any school in our system today. If you like and have the time, Jeff Becker, our resource officer, would be happy to give you a quick tour of the campus—"

"Oh, we wouldn't want to put him to the bother," Jim responded. "In any event, I have to get Don back downtown to the arena. He's supposed to be showing his company's flag on the exhibition hall floor this afternoon, and we only wanted to take a few minutes to see what the old place looked like."

"Well, it was so nice of you to drop in, even if it was for just a few minutes. Perhaps you'll come back when you have more time and let us show you around."

"That would be terrific. By the way, you wouldn't happen to remember a math teacher by the name of Peters, would you?"

"Peters? Peters? Why, yes. Gosh, I haven't heard that name in long time. As I recall, he retired about 20 years ago. I'm told the staff gave him quite a send-off."

"You wouldn't happen to have his last address, would you?" asked Don.

"Oh my gosh, I doubt it. And even if I did, I couldn't give it out. Personal security and all that. I'm sure you understand."

"Yes, of course. That's all right," responded Jim, "we'll find him if he's still around. Shouldn't take much."

With that, the men took their leave.

Once back in their car, Jim had a thought. "Wait a minute. You know, back in our senior year, I drove Mr. Peters home one brutally cold winter afternoon when we couldn't get his car started. As I recall, he lived with his parents—they had a big home; I mean, it was huge . . . Tudor Revival, if I recall—on Kenwood Boulevard, up near Lake Park Drive. Big money there, my friend. I distinctly remember being introduced to his mother when Mr. Peters invited me in for hot cocoa. Look up 'Raymond Peters' in the White Pages on your cell phone—"

"Way ahead of you," responded Don, showing Jim his phone. He's right where you said he was. It can't be more than ten minutes from here. Let's jump over there, say 'Hi,' and then, shoot downtown before I start feeling *really* guilty for taking all this time off."

"You got it!" said Jim, as he turned the car north and headed toward Kenwood Boulevard.

True to Don's estimate, the men soon were parked in front of Raymond Peter's home. The grass had yet to green up, but beds of daffodils already were poking their heads through the mulch beds next to the house, giving early signs that another beautiful Midwest spring was about to burst forth. The grounds were well attended, and the home still stood out among its peers on the block, not only as one of the finest examples of its architecture in the city, but also, as what the city's moneyed class had built in the early 1920s.

The men scrambled up the long walk to the front door and pressed the doorbell button. Then, they waited.

They rang again. They could hear the chimes.

The sound of the door being unlocked raised their spirits. Within seconds, they came face to face with Mr. Peters. "Yes?" inquired an elderly, hunched-over man seated in a wheelchair. "Is there something I can do for you?" Behind him stood a nurse's aide.

The men stared at him. This was not the Mr. Peters they had known and loved, the man who had taught them trigonometry, who once had that fire in his eyes—and in his belly—when it came to the field of mathematics and who, by the grace of God, had been able to transfer that gift to them and a few others in their class . . . the man who had shepherded them from math competition to math competition throughout their senior year, whose powers of concentration were so great that in his presence, they dared not even breathe while watching him solve some of the most difficult problems imaginable.

Oh. My. God, thought Don. *What happened to the Mr. Peters we knew?*

The men stood silent. "Frozen" might be a better descriptor.

Peters again asked: "Is there something I can do for you?"

Finally, Jim spoke. "Good afternoon, Mr. Peters, I'm Jim Reynolds. My friend Don Loman and I attended the high school on Locust Avenue where you taught many years ago."

"And now you're going to tell me," said Peters, "that I was your teacher."

"Well, yes, we were," replied Don, enthusiastically, hoping for some sign, *any sign*, of recognition from their old teacher.

"Sorry. I don't remember you." And with that, Peters backed his wheelchair, and shut and locked the door in their faces.

The men were stunned. Crestfallen, they turned and with mouths agape, looked at each other. Don shook his head. "What just happened?"

"I haven't the faintest," replied Jim.

They returned to their car and headed downtown, saying little.

"I guess it's true what they say," remarked Don, wistfully, as they pulled up to the arena.

"What's that?"

"You can't go home again."

Indeed, in the years that followed, Don never did return to Milwaukee; nor did he ever again give much thought to the days of his youth in the Cream City.

"Lost in the Library" (Photo: Brilliant Flash Fiction)
Librarian's Choice Writing Contest[3]

"I don't know why I ever listened to you," whispered Lindsay.

---

3 Contest closed May 30, 2020. There was no joy in Mudville, unfortunately.

33. Lost in the Library

Theodore Jerome Cohen

"I don't know why I ever listened to you," whispered Lindsay, as if anyone even could have heard her at 11 p.m. in the library of a small community college located several miles east of Holcomb, Kansas. "Oh, don't be such a killjoy," Alexa replied. "You could have said 'No' when I asked if you wanted to join the scavenger hunt my sorority was sponsoring tonight. As I recall, you were rather excited about it."

"Yeah, but I didn't expect it would involve breaking into the college library. Stopping strangers on the street to ask if they had a $2 bill or driving to the men's dorms in search of a St. Patrick's Day hat is one thing, but this is crazy. I'm still trying to figure out how we ended up losing ourselves here, on the second floor. The only thing we were given was a Post-It Note with '364' and the demand to 'Bring back information on the killers' scribbled on it."

"Well, to my mind, this meant finding either a location in town with an address of '364' in which some killers live or lived—fat chance of that—or finding a relevant murder mystery in the library under the 364-call number using the Dewey Decimal System. So, in a way, we're not *really* lost."

Lindsay rolled her eyes. "Give me a break. Just because you're a Library Science major doesn't mean every time you see a three-digit number, visions of books in a library should pop in your head. What's so special about the number 364 anyway?"

"Well, for one thing, in library speak, it connotes Criminology," said Alexa.

"Okay, I get it, I get it."

"Now, what's the date today?" Alexa could barely contain her glee in asking this question.

"November 15th."

"And what's the nearest town to the west?"

"Holcomb."

"So?"

"So?" Lindsay gave her friend a blank look.

"Sheesh." An exasperated look crossed Alexa's face. "I see I'm gonna have to show you. Follow me."

With that, she began walking down the aisle, Lindsay in tow. Using a tiny flashlight linked to her key chain for illumination, and letting her forefinger bump from volume to volume on the middle bookshelf, Alexa studied the number printed on the small white label affixed to each book's spine.

Here and there she paused before moving on until she came upon a book with the call number 364.1/523. It was a thick volume wedged tightly between the books on either side. Using her hands to pry the books apart, she gently eased a well-worn copy of Truman Capote's *In Cold Blood* from the shelf and handed it to Lindsay.

"Is this what we've been looking for?" Lindsay asked.

Alexa nodded. "I'm sure this is what we need to complete the hunt. The number we were given, today's date, our proximity to Holcomb . . . it all makes sense. Twenty years ago, to the day, two men—Perry Smith and Richard Hickock—murdered Herb Clutter, his wife, and their two teenage kids in Holcomb. All we need to do now is execute—no pun intended—a little midnight requisition of this book, and— What's wrong, Lindsay? You look like you've seen a ghost!"

Lindsay stood frozen; her head tilted to one side. "Did you hear something?"

"No. Did you?"

"Yes! I heard footsteps behind me."

"Oh, come on, Lindsay—"

"There they are again," she said, a look of terror on her face. "I'm sure of it. Let's get outta here!" She turned and bolted for the back of the library, for the window through which they had entered.

Alexa, following in hot pursuit, watched as she turned and disappeared at the end of the aisle. But as Alexa turned the corner and approached the window, Lindsay was nowhere to be seen.

"Lindsay!" she whispered, clutching Capote's book to her chest. "Where are you?"

There was no answer.

"Come on, Lindsay," she whispered emphatically. "Quit screwin' around. Where are you? You couldn't have gotten lost!"

Then she, too, heard footsteps behind her.

91

"Days of Jealousy, Nights of Anger" (Photo: Paula)

"They'll be coming soon, you know."

34. Days of Jealousy, Nights of Anger

Theodore Jerome Cohen

"They'll be coming soon, you know," she said, staring out her dorm room window.

"Who'll be coming?" I asked, raising my gaze over the top of the magazine I was reading, one of many I had found strewn about the floor next to her bed.

She didn't answer. Instead, she continued to stare blankly into the mixture of sleet and rain that pelted the glass panes in front of her early on this Sunday evening in late February.

Allison had driven more than 150 miles earlier that afternoon while returning to college, having spent the previous day—and night—with Ryan, her boyfriend of many years. Not that they hadn't know each other practically since birth.

They were born with days of each other at the community hospital and lived their entire lives on the same block in a small town in upstate Vermont. Their parents knew each other, as well and, in fact, socialized together. To say Allison and Ryan were good friends through grade school and the first two years of high school would be an understatement.

But then, the girl who had been slow to mature physically and was chronically shy began to blossom into a beautiful young woman who caught the attention of a blonde, blue-eyed boy who, during the summer following his sophomore year, shot up to 6' 2", added muscles where there had been none before, a slight mustache, low voice, and to everyone's surprise, made the varsity football team at their high school.

Now, friends became lovers, and the two were inseparable, so much so that when it came time to select colleges, both decided upon a small institution in the Midwest where Ryan could pursue his interest in sports education while Allison focused on biology with a view toward pre-med. On weekends, his love of sports frequently took them to the Big Ten university 160 miles to the south for that institution's football and basketball games—something that, by the end of his freshman year, reignited Ryan's desire to participate actively in sports.

There was only one thing for him to do: transfer that Big Ten university, which he did at the end of his sophomore year.

Allison was heartsick. Contemplating even a day without seeing Ryan was something she dreaded. Now, she knew there would *weeks* when she couldn't see him.

"Don't worry," he said late one summer evening before they both left for their junior years. "We'll be able to talk every night—hell, we'll probably talk several times each day! And we'll see each other on weekends and holidays. I'll be up to see you. And I'm sure, knowing you, you'll be driving down to see me. Meanwhile, we'll both be doing the things we love and preparing for our future together."

It all *sounded* good to her, but a little voice in the back of her head told her too many things could go wrong. She thought about several of her friends who had seen their relationships "blow up" when their "steadies" went off to school and met another person. Or when one or another in a relationship were separated for a long period of time—for whatever reason—and were never able to rekindle what they had had before the separation. No, too many things could go wrong, of that she was sure, and all the assurances in the world from Ryan did nothing to assuage her feelings.

Still, what could she do?

She returned to college in the fall and threw herself into her work. At first, it was as he said; they talked frequently throughout the day and at times, long into the night. And yes, there were those weekends together, at his university as well as at her college. It wasn't like when they both attended the same school, but still, as time went on, her anxiety eased and she took comfort in believing they could make it work.

But then, old doubts started to rear their heads again. Why didn't Ryan answer his cell phone immediately when she called? Why, at times, did he seem distracted when they were talking, as if there were something else—*or someone else*—in the room vying for his attention? Why did he ask her to change her plans at the last minute—to come down the following weekend instead of the weekend they had planned to meet only a few days earlier?

Her suspicions rose, as did her anger. They were her demons in the night.

Finally, near midnight one weekday, she drove to his apartment to surprise him. She was determined, once and for all, either to put her suspicions to rest or catch him in the act of sleeping with someone else.

Fortunately for Ryan, his roommate had been up late studying for a mid-term exam. He chanced to see Allison pull into a parking space outside their apartment at 3:00 a.m. Waking Ryan, the two men rushed Elise, the football team's equipment manager, from Ryan's bed into his roommate's bedroom before Allison, using her key, entered the apartment. Satisfied no one else was there, she and Ryan spent the night together while Ryan's roommate let Elise sleep in his bed, waking her before dawn to drive her back to her dorm.

As calming to her as that trip might have been, it was only a week later, when she was FaceTiming Ryan, that Allison was startled to see Elise suddenly appear behind him on her cell phone's screen!

"How did *she* get in?!" Allison demanded to know.

Ryan, stumbling for words, made a lame excuse about having left the apartment door unlocked. In truth, Elise had her own key. Meanwhile, quick to recover from this embarrassing moment, Elise quickly handed Ryan her English lit notes, asking him to "[p]lease double-check my football equipment database to make sure I haven't made a mistake on your body measurements."

Allison didn't "buy it." Later, in another call, she told Ryan, in no uncertain terms, Elise was going to be the death of him.

Now, she rose slowly from the window and walked to her vanity. There, she sat and as the unmistakable sounds of police sirens began penetrating the silence of her dorm room, she slowly brushed her hair.

"I told you they'd be coming," she said matter-of-factly, putting down her hairbrush and picking up her lipstick.

"Comet" (Photo: K. S. Brooks)
Indies Unlimited, July 18, 2020[4]

**"This is the perfect spot from which to view the comet.
Isn't she beautiful?"**

---

4 Though the photo prompt is from Indies Unlimited's weekly competition for July 18, 2020, the story was too long to submit for competition. That said, I thank Ms. Brooks for inspiring me to write this tale.

35. Comet

Theodore Jerome Cohen

"Doctor Atkins? Is that *you?*"

The elderly gentleman—Professor Jonathan Atkins of the University of Wisconsin-Madison's Department of English Literature, who moments earlier had been staring over Lake Mendota at the Comet NEOWISE—quickly slipped on his COVID-19 protective mask and turned to recognize a familiar face from his online summer school class on classical poetry.

"Well, well, Meredith Reynolds. What a nice surprise to see you here!" he said, nodding to her and the young man by her side.

"Doctor Atkins, this is my fiancé, Jim Butler. He's working on his Ph.D. in biotechnology. We have a small apartment on State Street, up near the capitol."

"Evening, Professor," the young man said, bringing his mask to his face after being jabbed in the side by his soon-to-be wife.

"And a good evening to you, as well," the professor said. "I should have known others would join me at the end of North Francis Street. This is the perfect spot from which to view the comet. Isn't she beautiful? Better catch her now, though! We won't have another chance for 6800 years." He chuckled at his own joke.

"You know," remarked the professor, comets were often thought of as portending significant events . . . signaling, if you will, something good—or bad—had happened or was about to happen. Does this bring anything to mind, Meredith?"

This is where the rubber hits the road, the professor thought to himself. For more than a month he and his class had been studying Virgil's *Eclogues,* a group of ten poems modeled on the pastoral poetry of the Hellenistic poet Theocritus.

If he were to be asked, Meredith was his best student. In a word, she was a "joy" to teach. Her homework always was completed on time, her contributions to the online classes were many and insightful, and she often steered the conversation in directions even the professor had not thought to explore. Now, he was putting her on the spot. A bit unfair, to be sure, for the portion of the poem he had in mind was obscure yet still relevant to the moment.

Meredith threw her head back and looked him square in the eye. "That's an interesting question, Professor. I suspect you're trying to have a little fun at my expense?"

"Why Meredith, I would *never* do that," he said, winking at her fiancé.

"Well, let's see," she said. "I think you're referring to Virgil's ninth eclogue, in which he wrote about the star of Caesar appearing to gladden the field."

"I'm impressed," said Atkins.

"Would I get extra credit," asked his star pupil, "if I also told you Virgil wrote the following about the period following Caesar's assassination: 'Never did fearsome comets so often blaze'?"

Atkins threw his arms into the air. "I surrender!" he shouted to peals of laughter from the couple. "Yes, you get the extra credit. In fact, you get an 'A' for the course. Just keep showing up for our online classes and providing your valuable insights.

"After all, you are *my* shining star!"

"Tunnel" Photo: K. S. Brooks
Indies Unlimited, September 19, 2020

The two Notre Dame alumni . . . stood at the head-end of the tunnel.

36. Tunnel

Theodore Jerome Cohen

The two Notre Dame alumni, members of the university's last championship football team, the Fighting Irish of 1988, stood at the head-end of the tunnel, quietly staring down its length to the field that had awaited them so many times decades earlier. Cigars in hand, neither said a word, apparently lost in their memories of those glorious days and the men with whom they played. They almost certainly were thinking about the ones who had passed: Bob Satterfield, Jeff Alm, Rodney Culver, Kenny Spears, Andre Jones, and now, only a few days earlier, Dean Brown.

"I still can't believe Dean's gone," said one, breaking his silence after taking a puff on his cigar. "I talked with his brother the night he went to the Cleveland Clinic. He said Dean thought he some kind of respiratory infection. He even texted his wife from the ER, saying he might be discharged soon. But he died later that day of a blood clot."

His team member nodded. "Doesn't seem fair, does it?! I mean, the guy was 44 years old. He was in the prime of his life."

"I know, but look at Andre; he was only 27 when he died from a brain tumor."

Taking one last look at the tunnel, they turned and walked through the stadium to their car.

"You know," said the driver, "back in 1988, we never knew a loss; we were on top of the world. Look what's happened to us now."

"Braids" (Photo: lotos foto, Bigstock Photo)

**"I thought we had an agreement you were *not* going
to torment Gertrude by pulling on her braids."**

37. Braids

Theodore Jerome Cohen

"What year is this, Mr. Stone?"
"It's 1948, Mr. Manske, sir."
"So, that would make you . . . ?"
"Ten years old, sir?"

"Ah, yes. Ten years old. And quite the young man, wouldn't you say so, Mr. Stone?"

"I-I guess so, Mr. Manske."

"So, tell me, Mr. Stone: why is this the second time this month Miss Stark has sent you to the principal's office to discuss your behavior in class?"

[Silence]

"Let me help you, Mr. Stone. Might it have something to do with Gertrude, the girl who sits at the desk in front of you? Something related to how you've been annoying Gertrude while Miss Stark is teaching class?"

"Well, Gertrude's always starting it, Mr. Manske!"

"We've talked about this before, Mr. Stone, and I thought we'd come to an understanding about the part you've been playing in this matter."

"Yes, sir."

"I thought you had agreed you were going to refrain— Let me reword that. I thought we had an agreement you were *not* going to torment Gertrude by pulling on her braids."

"Yes, sir. But she's always swishing them back and forth. And sometimes, when I'm writing with my ink pen, her braids smear my writing."

"I understand how that can make you angry, Mr. Stone. But instead of yanking on her braids, wouldn't it be better simply to raise your hand and ask Miss Stark to help you and Gertrude work things out?"

"I'll try next time, Mr. Manske. Really. I promise I will."

"I certainly hope so, young man. Sticking the tips of Gertrude's braids in your ink bottle certainly is *not* a good way to make things better!"

"506" (Photo: (K. S. Brooks)
Indies Unlimited, May 29, 2021[5]

"If it's any help, the address we had on file for Celestia's family is 506 McClellan Lane, here in Syracuse."

---

5 Though the photo prompt is from Indies Unlimited's weekly competition for May 29, 2021, the story was too long to submit for competition. That said, I thank Ms. Brooks for inspiring me to write this tale.

38. 506
Theodore Jerome Cohen

"Does the name Tia or Celestia ring a bell?" asked NYPD Homicide Detective Lou Martelli. He was on his cell phone talking to Edward Lane, Principal, Marquis de Lafayette High School.

"Oh, yes, of course," replied Lane. "Very bright young lady. Attractive, too. As I recall, she was here under a scholarship provided by an anonymous benefactor. Unfortunately, Tia left in the middle of her junior year. I must say, it was quite unexpected."

"How so?"

"Well, one day, her father just walked into my office and abruptly pulled her out of school . . . said something about his being transferred out-of-country. The family was gone two days later, lock, stock, and barrel. No one ever saw them again. Nor did anyone ever learn what happened to her or her family. They simply vanished into thin air."

"Who did the father work for?"

"I haven't a clue . . . and before you ask, no, our records wouldn't show that kind of information. Yes, they would show a student's emergency contact names, address, and telephone numbers, but in most cases, these would almost always be their parent's names and home telephone or cell phone numbers."

Lane paused while he consulted his computer files. "If it's any help, the address we had on file for Celestia's family is 506 McClellan Lane, here in Syracuse.

"I recall her mother was a stay-at-home mom because there were two much younger children in the family. We talked about them briefly on one parent-teacher's night at the high school."

Martelli thought for a moment. "Ed, when I was in high school, we had a photography club. Do you have one?"

"You bet, one of the best in the area."

"So, there were always lots of guys and gals taking photographs of just about anything and everything throughout the school year, and maybe into the summer?"

"Absolutely. In fact, we used to do most of our own film developing and printing using the old dark room in the basement of the administration building. Posted many of the club's photos on the bulletin boards throughout the school. Still do, in fact, though today everything is digital. We also use these photos in the school newspaper, for event publicity offsite—for example, on the bulletin boards at the local grocery and drug stores—and in our yearbooks."

"So, it's safe to assume Tia appears in some of these photos, whether on purpose or by accident."

"I would think so, Detective."

"Ed, this is very important. You may be one of the few people who not only remember Tia, but also, who remember what she looks like.

"I know this may be an imposition, but could I ask you, for starters, to go through the school newspapers and photos for the years in which Tia was a student. If you find any pictures of her, any pictures at all, regardless of their size and quality, please make copies using your cell phone and e-mail them to me. It's vital we find this woman.

"I wish I could tell you more. Perhaps someday I'll be in a position to do that. But for now, trust me when I tell you she may hold the key to our understanding of what happened to her classmates, Trent Morrison and Brent Hallaway."

Lane didn't immediately respond. In fact, for a moment, Martelli thought he had lost the connection.

"Ed? Ed? Are you still there?"

"Yes, I'm still here, Detective. I don't know if I can do what you ask. Don't you need some kind of warrant to obtain those pictures? I mean, first of all, the pictures are of minors. And second, the photos are the property of a private institution—this high school."

"I understand your concerns, Ed. But as you said, many of the pictures are already in the public domain, so to speak, by having been published in the school newspaper, which certainly must have been taken outside the school, or by having been posted in stores around the local neighborhood.

"Now, we could get a judge to issue a warrant, if that's required. But frankly, if the press got wind of that, think what might happen when they start poking around. You certainly don't need the publicity, let alone the interruptions. And believe me, the press can be relentless . . . and ruthless. If there's even the whiff—"

"I get it, Detective. I'll do as you ask and be in contact as soon as I have something."

"And Ed—"

"Yes?"

"I don't have to tell you how sensitive this is. So, please keep this just between us."

"I understand. You can count on me. I'll start looking through the school's newspapers and other photos as soon as we hang up."

Martelli's partner, Detective-Specialist Sean O'Keeffe, sat silently through the entire exchange between Martelli and Ed Lane. He could hear both sides of the conversation. When his partner finally ended the call and put his cell phone on the seat next to him, O'Keeffe turned to him and chuckled. "I got news for you, Buddy. You don't stand a snowball's chance in Hell of finding that woman. I don't care if Ed gives you a thousand pictures of her—they could even have been taken yesterday—she'll never be found."

"What the hell are you talking about, Sean?"

"She's in the witness protection program, Lou."

See Endnote 6.

Endnotes

1. **The Doves Type**

¶ THE DOVES TYPE® is Robert Green's digital
recreation of the Doves Press Fount of Type.

Original type conceived, commissioned & directed
by T. J. Cobden-Sanderson, London, 1899.

Developed by Emery Walker, assisted by Percy Tiffin,
at Walker & Boutall, London, 1899 — 1900.

Punches cut by Edward Prince, London, 1899 — 1901.

Produced in a single size, 2 Line Brevier (16 pt),
by Miller & Richard, Edinburgh, 1899 — 1905.

First sorts delivered October 1899, full fount of
characters completed July 1901.

Punches & matrices thrown into the River Thames
by T. J. Cobden-Sanderson, March 1913.

Entire type dropped into the River Thames by
T. J. Cobden-Sanderson, August 1916 — January 1917.

Digital facsimile Doves Type® developed 2010 — 2015.

OpenType Version 1.0 released December 2013.
Version 2.0 released January 2015.

Created using sources from original Doves Press
publications & 150 metal sorts recovered from the
River Thames by Robert Green & the Port of London
Authority salvage team, October & November 2014.

The Doves Type® — www.dovestype.com

Distributed by Typespec Ltd — www.typespec.co.uk

2. Set a Place for Sister Margaret
This story was first published in the *CQ* magazine (Amateur Radio, Communications & Technology), March/April, 2014, p. 88.

3. Falls
Anyone who's read Lewis Carroll's (aka Charles Lutwidge Dodgson's) *Alice in Wonderland* and others of Carroll's *Alice* books will instantly recognize Charles, the Reverend Robinson Duckworth (aka "the Duck"), and the Liddell sisters: Lorina, Alice, and Edith. Three entries from June, 1863, were cut from the diaries of Charles Dodgson by his heirs. Importantly, in the pages that followed, he no longer socialized with the Liddells.

4. Spring Fling
This story was inspired by the life—and death--of Ted and Susan's friend, Army Captain James F. "Jimmy" Adamouski. Ted's novel, *Eighth Circle: A Special Place in Hell,* is dedicated to Jimmy. You can learn more about this book at:

https://www.theodore-cohen-novels.com/eighthcircle.html

Ted's *Flash Fiction Stories of the Warrier* also is dedicated to Jimmy:

https://www.theodore-cohen-novels.com/creativeinkflashyfiction9.html

Both books may be found on Amazon, B&N, and Kobo.

Jimmy's remains were buried with full military honors in Arlington National Cemetery and West Point Cemetery.

5. Fraternity Prank
Someone *did* make a film about Delta Tau Chi. It's called *Animal House,* and today, it's considered a classic. You can view the trailer here:

https://www.youtube.com/watch?v=m8psQi7ScQQ

6. 506

This story, based on facts, was excerpted from, and modified after, Ted's fourth novel in his NYPD Detective Louis Martelli, NYPD, Mystery/Thriller Series, *Night Shadows*. For more information on this book, see:

https://www.theodore-cohen-novels.com/nightshadows.html

The book is available in Kindle, paperback, and audiobook editions from Amazon:

https://www.amazon.com/dp/B00J828Q20

As well, it can be found on B&N in paperback and Nook, and on Kobo:

https://www.barnesandnoble.com/w/night-shadows-theodore-cohen/1118958347?ean=9780984920983

https://www.kobo.com/us/en/ebook/night-shadows-15

Books in this series can be read in any order.

About the Authors

Theodore Jerome (Ted) Cohen is an award-winning author who has published more than ten novels—all but one of them mystery/thrillers—and two books of short stories. This is his fifteenth book in his <u>Flash Fiction Anthology</u> series. He also writes illustrated storybooks for children (K-3) in the series <u>Stories for the Early Years</u>. Dr. Cohen holds three degrees in the physical sciences from the University of Wisconsin – Madison. During the course of his 45-year career he worked as an engineer, scientist, CBS Radio Station News Service (RSNS) commentator, private investigator, and Antarctic explorer. What he's been able to do with his background is mix fiction with reality in ways that even his family and friends have been unable to unravel!

Dr. Cohen's writings (he holds three degrees in the physical sciences from the University of Wisconsin – Madison) have received the highest reviews from Feathered Quill, Hollywood Book Reviews, Kirkus Discoveries, Pacific Book Review, Reader Views, and Readers' Favorite, among others, with many of his books recognized for their excellence through medals awarded by several of these same organizations following their annual book competitions. In 2017, for example, Readers' Favorite awarded Dr. Cohen's first short story anthology, *The Road Less Taken: A Collection of* Unusual *Short Stories - Book 1*, a Silver Medal while the National Association of Book Entrepreneurs (NABE) awarded the same book its Pinnacle Book Achievement Award for Best in Category: Short Stories. A member of the Society of Children's Book Writers and Illustrators (SCBWI), Dr. Cohen's articles often can be found in that organization's *BULLETIN* as well as in *Story Monsters Ink* magazine.

From December 1961 through early March 1962, Dr. Cohen participated in the 16th Chilean Expedition to the Antarctic. The US Board of Geographic Names in October, 1964, named the geographical feature Cohen Islands, located at 63° 18' S. latitude, 57° 53' W. longitude in the Cape Legoupil area, Antarctica, in his honor. And given he is an avid communicator (Dr. Cohen has been a licensed Radio Amateur since 1952, and holds an Amateur Extra Class license (call sign: N4XX)) and an accomplished violinist (he played with the Bryn Athyn (PA) Orchestra from 2007 through 2013), it is not unexpected that stories involving the Antarctic, radio, and music are to be found throughout his writings.

In addition to his adult and childrens books, Dr. Cohen writes Young Adult (YA) novels under the pen name Alyssa Devine. His YA novel *The Hypnotist* (Lexile® measure 930L) currently is in the Core Genre (Mystery) Reading Program at Neshaminy High School in Bucks County, Pennsylvania, where he is a guest lecturer on the subject of mystery writing.

Finally, from March 1966, through March, 1968, Dr. Cohen served as a Captain in the United States Army, Corps of Engineers.

Dr. Cohen and his wife, Susan, live in southeastern Pennsylvania, not far from where Washington crossed the Delaware River to surprise the Hessian forces in Trenton, New Jersey, on the night of December 25-26, 1776. Visit Ted at <www.theodore-cohen-novels.com>.

Alyssa Devine is the pseudonym Dr. Cohen uses for the award-winning author of Young Adult (YA) mystery/thrillers, police procedurals, and selected Flash Fiction tales. Among other things, "her" books and short stories explore the paranormal, tarot card readings, reincarnation, and magical realism. In her novels, readers will discover contemporaneously realistic stories about teenagers in settings similar to those found in their own homes, schools, and towns. For information on Alyssa Devine's writings, you are invited to visit <www.alyssadevinenovels.com>.